THE DEATH OF THE NOVEL AND OTHER STORIES

Books by Ronald Sukenick

THE DEATH OF THE NOVEL AND OTHER STORIES

UP

WALLACE STEVENS: MUSING THE OBSCURE

THE DEATH OF THE NOVEL AND OTHER STORIES

by
RONALD SUKENICK

 THE DIAL PRESS, INC.
NEW YORK 1969

Grateful acknowledgment is made to the following magazines in whose pages some of these stories first appeared: *Epoch,* Fall 1960 for "Permanent Crisis" and *The Paris Review,* No. 44, Fall 1968 for "What's Your Story"

For my collaborators, who walk in and out of these stories

"Roast Beef: A Slice of Life" was done in collaboration with Lynn
Luria Sukenick

TABLE
OF CONTENTS

THE PERMANENT CRISIS

If it was true that when last night before his desk he sat head on veiny forearms, a very young man though ordinarily as capable as most people at that moment as helpless as most people, until Honey called from the other room—the bedroom—it was the third time, Come to bed, without getting an answer for the third time, and again, Come to *bed,* and he raised his head, roared, NO, then lowered it onto his fist propped elbow on desk, staring at his blank page with an expression that looked like the mask of misery, saying to himself, it's like being in space so empty you don't even know whether you're there, trying to describe what was happening so it would stop happening, this paralysis, to call it a paralysis, because he would know what to think about it and more important, what to feel about it, and she came to the door of the bedroom and moaned, What are you doing? in her blue pajamas and the single long braid of thick brown hair that she slept in coming over her shoulder, falling like a brush between her breasts, sleepy, cranky, eyes half closed and cheeks flushed from the warmth of bed, and he answered, I'm laying an egg, she opened her eyes to a wide, fuzzy, unfocused, sleepy, guileless brown, asking, You're what?

I'm laying an EGG, and her eyes opened a little wider and she turned and fled back to the bedroom her braid trailing behind, like a chinaman, or a furry animal, but was standing in the door-way again an instant later, more angry than hurt shouting, Don't yell at me, stamping her bare foot on the floor at "yell," and when he heard the springs creak as she dived back into bed (he

1

could imagine it exactly), he was already thinking, like the loss
of ambition no, like the exhaustion of desire no, more, as if he
couldn't discover the forms for desire, or as if he wanted nothing
because he could find nothing to want, or—but she came to
disturb his formulations again, going timidly to sit in the easy
chair across from his desk but not speaking, not even looking at
him, just drawing her legs onto the chair and sitting quietly with
an unhappy expression and her body quivering slightly, from tension maybe, or from fatigue, until he glared at her curled in the
chair and she looked up nervously, looked down, then looked up
again eyes widened unhappily asking, Is it the cat?—the cat, they
had had an argument about the cat, The cat, he replied, will
have to go.

You know you said before we were married that I could keep
my cat.

It's not the cat.

I don't care about the cat.

Why don't you go to sleep?

I can't sleep. I'm lonely. You make me feel lonely.

Well if it was a mistake it's not too late for an annulment, he
said and was sorry as soon as he looked at her, though it was in
his mind and had been for quite a while, though he had never
really accepted being married, never really decided to get married, but one day after he had been sleeping with her for a long
time without ever having mentioned it before, without ever saying
that he was in love with her or even, as far as he could remember,
mentioning that he was fond of her, when he was pleased with his
life and with the world he suddenly (it was a surprise to himself)
said, What do you say we get married? and she without taking
time to breathe or blink answered Yes, and a little stunned he
asked, How come you say yes so quickly? immediately regretting
he had asked but after flinching at the question she answered,
Because I'm tired of saying no, so that he had to laugh and then
she laughed but nevertheless since he had proposed because he
felt good he was never sure it wasn't a mistake when he felt bad
except that from the first time he took her to bed he never
troubled much to doubt he was in whatever love was with her, so
that he said to her in grudging apology, I feel bad. It has nothing
to do with you.

That's why I feel lonely, she answered quickly, a just remark he felt since in the last months it had all been disappearing, his work, his degree, his career—not that they weren't still there, but that he couldn't see them, a death of interest—disappearing, disappeared, until tonight he felt he too could disappear, like a rocket to space, pushing off with rush and energy to break through and find nothing there, last seen floating in the direction of the sun, a death of interest, that was it, Is it something that happened? she asked, and he thought and tried to answer with evident sanity though if it were insane it would be better in a way because there was always the nearest analyst, something—who knows?—he might come to anyway as half of the people he knew already had, and some of the others ought to, Yes, no, yes. That is, yes, something seems to be happening. I'm failing. Everything is slipping through my fingers.

But how, failing? You're first in your school . . .

And the right job waiting for me, the one I wanted, and a wife to be envied, everything on schedule and altogether an august personage, no. Life is failure. Or if that's not true, that's the way I feel, or he wondered, did that sound hollow, what had he expected that the enlightened, liberal upper middle class wasn't going to give him, what life freer, larger that he had sensed since long ago beyond his home, beyond the reach of his family, beyond the imagination of his father, that good man, with his store failed in Williamsburg, failed in Flatbush, failed in Bensonhurst, failing in every drab corner of Brooklyn, failed once, even, in Canarsie, and then the war when he made money, a lot of it, lost Eugene in Belgium and finally retired guilt-stricken, well-off to die—what it amounted to—of confusion, what life that he had conceived, whose immense possibilities he had been led to conceive by the mouthings of the least grammar school teacher, by the large noises of an entire culture, of intelligent effort and dignified fulfillment, of dignity, yes, what life that as he had known for a long time through simple observation did not for him exist, or not as represented, that he knew he was going to hate—which he might have put up with—but that he suddenly felt as empty, as tawdry, and above all, as pointless as the succession of stores in Brooklyn only worse, because you would have to know exactly what you were doing to yourself, But why? she asked, Why?

It's like there's some kind of fraud going on, I don't know. I feel like I've been promised too much, and the hell of it is, I still expect it.

But you're not making sense. Why fraud?

Because I feel cheated.

Of what? The world is wide open. There are lots of things you can do with a law degree.

So they say, but it was more than a sense of being swindled, it was like a feeling of betraying something—but what? since there was nothing to betray in a society in whose forms and procedures he neither believed nor disbelieved but to which he would be committed above all as a lawyer, catching him in a pattern of guilt he felt working already and which he felt powerless to change, in which success would aggravate rebellion and rebellion would bring success because that was what they wanted, to be told what was wrong, to get the disease named and the guilt isolated— this gluttony for medicine that was itself a disease—a process that would take and take but never give, finally leaving him utterly to himself, as he was now, a bug caught and squirming on its own pin, I'm going to secede, I'm leaving, he told her,

To go where?

You tell me. Nowhere, leaving him utterly to himself, that was it, a self that could only analyze its own consciousness, a consciousness aware only of its own muttering, It's after three, she interrupted dolorously and he noticed that the pout around the corners of her lips had collapsed to a look of patient despair and didn't answer her until she added, Do you want to talk about it?

It's not a matter of talking about it.

You're just feeling bad.

You're a genius. Straight to the heart of things every time.

Please tell me what I can do.

Leave me alone, he told her, and she blinked and sighed but stayed in her chair, and he thought, it's as if everything in the world looked like New Jersey;

it was also true that the cat came out of its corner and he watched it glide across the carpet, malign beast, that he had been waking up to find in the bed, on the pillow, its fur in his face, that filled the apartment with its odors, that today, last straw, had

shredded his tort and apparently eaten page seven, to rub its pearl-
blue back which was he had to admit beautiful against the leg of
his wife's chair, that it stretched to a long arabesque, turned,
curved back along the chair, looked, arched, sprang, and curled
itself into the warmth of her lap, that he got up and went into the
kitchen, coming back for no reason with an opened can of sardines in his hand, placed it at the foot of his wife's chair saying,
Cats like sardines, and she suddenly looked up, startled, saying,
Oh my god, my sardines, snatching them up just as the cat leaped
down, That's my lunch, putting them on his desk, then reached
out picking one from the can with her fingers saying I like sardines, eating from her hand, licked her fingers, then reached out
for another, as he had done once—where was it?—when he had
lived for two weeks on sardines and Wheaties until some nice girl
had come along to among other things feed him, Chicago, and
then some money had come, he took a sardine, ate it and discovered he was hungry, or was it L.A., the hotel permeated by
the smell of urine like rotting spinach, no Chicago where he was
going to college that time because L.A. was only a trip with
Banally that crass son of a bitch who never believed anything and
took it for granted no questions asked and who drove off and left
him stranded in of all places Needles, California because he was
trying to make some girl he had picked up and he got back hitch-
hiking to Chicago just in time to pack up and move to Boston,
You want to get that bread? he asked her, to start the school year
because he was following the money then and somebody was
offering him more in Boston where he almost married black-eyed
Lillian, it would have been easier to take rat poison, faster and
less painful, she came back with the bread and a knife and they
finished the sardines, cutting off the bread in chunks, just before
he had finished his degree when he left for New York in a bad
mood that got worse for a year of nothing where tired of living on
part-time jobs and his mother's money he tried law school with
the idea of making a life and stuck to the grind not because he
liked it but because he discovered he could do it, a life with some
kind of sense to it and maybe do some of the things he liked and
complain about some he didn't or at least make enough money to
be left alone in some sort of as he had imagined it dignified
abstention, alone at least with his own griefs, if that was possible,
which it wasn't, he sliced off a piece of bread, started to eat it, and

wanted a drink, probably the sardines, went to the kitchen bringing back the bourbon and a couple of glasses which he set on the
desk, Just a little, she said, to keep you company, and was
grinding away not thinking of anything except getting the damn
thing over with when he met Roberta whom he later came to call
Honey—he remembered why and when—and ended by marrying
her, he gulped his drink, she was sipping and playing with hers,
didn't really want it, without ever deciding to get married, as if
everything had added up to that and decided for him before he
had known it, but going on the idea after it had happened that if
nothing else you could enjoy life as his grandfather used to tell
him, Live! Enjoy! giving him nickels which his mother always
made him put in his little bank, that old goat-faced bastard who
arrived from one of the gayer metropoli of the dolorous old
country landing in the middle of the Gilded Age and going spats
and cane through war, depression, and war without getting
noticeably disturbed, brutally selfish, and who died no doubt
without a regret having apparently consumed all the joy of his
family for a generation and happened to be the only member of
it who ever appealed to him, and here he was with degree, job,
wife, and sad as all hell, wondering why all this was coming
together now, what he had done, was doing, noticed his wife
nodding in her chair, her thick lashes veiling her eyes, wondering
why it was all coming together what he had done, where he had
been, the people, the girls who had always sooner or later turned
up, how he had been alone in cities and something had always
turned up, a friend or someone with a car and money always
coming from somewhere and the Coast when he got sick of Chicago and New York when he got sick of Boston, how there was
always some other place to go and even something else to do and
misery wherever he had been whatever he had been doing always
come and always gone away, how it all came together and was a
life, some kind of life, he saw his wife almost asleep sprawling in
her chair a little childishly and could have kissed her, probably
the drink, that he never knew how he was going to feel tomorrow
but tonight there were still places he wanted to see and things he
wanted to find out about and work he wanted to do, wondered
why he suddenly wanted to kiss her and did, saying, Don't say
I'm never nice to you.

No, it's not every man who gets around to kissing his wife,

she answered, but was pleased, and if it's so tonight it might be so again tomorrow and if not tomorrow then the day after, and he stopped trying to figure it out, playing it by ear, listening to himself because there was nothing else to listen to and it sounded right he wondered why, as if he were some kind of artist and knew he was right but didn't know how he knew, he would have to write that down, Are you getting sleepy? she asked trying not to sound too eager,

Yeah.

Do you want to come to bed?

Yeah.

How come? she asked, surprised and he grinned, saying, Because I'm tired of saying no.

That must be the first time in a week.

What?

That you smiled at me, he wondered why because nothing had changed and he had no faith in that life he knew was going to make him betray something (but what?) he couldn't betray and leave him in the end to himself, and that he had to fail, Let's go, he said and turned out one light, that he knew he was already caught in it, born into it, he turned out the second light, and that all he could do was listen to himself and improvise, he would have to write that down on his page, like an improvisation again and again and never the same, he led her into the bedroom, and yes, if he expected too much then he preferred it, if it was pointless then it was pointless, if he was disintegrated all right he was disintegrated, he turned out the last light, because he knew this was going to happen to him again and again no matter what and all he could do was try to sense what was happening and compose it like a man as he listens to his own voice composing ceaselessly, he would have to write this down all of it, within a flood which even as he embraced that warmth wondering while he still had time if he couldn't write the whole thing down to have at least the words to repeat and understand swept him beyond his words of it.

MOMENTUM

His room in the slum.

This is perhaps naive;
distortion occurs in
    the moment
as in memory;
the mind is quick
the feelings quicker;
but I want the moment
    live
in its dishonesty,
minimal affectation:
correction in re-
flection.

More: constriction of
life paralysis of
    vitality—
the garotte of the slum,
the garret of the mind.

Tunnel—skyline: N.Y.'s
tight rectumtangles.

   okay here we go   i don't want to
whisper this   i want to hear my nat
ural speaking voice   the way it really
sounds   also i can see myself here in
a full-length mirror as i speak   there's
another mirror too   so that i can't
really lose sight of myself as i sit down
on my bed or lie down or walk around
   i want to say this as it comes with
out premeditation because i want to
say it before i lose it   or not so much
say it as tell it   tell it to myself so i'll
have it down   so that i can come
back to it again and recapture it   so
the speed of the tape is my form
keep talking as the tape records   non
stop   tuesday   it wasn't merely that i
had to go up there to find a place for
us to live in the summer   i had been
in a condition of somnolence   stupor
perhaps more like it   going to bed
late at night   three or four   getting
ten hours sleep   waking up toward
noon or past   one o'clock sometimes
   and i wanted to break that   i got to
the bus station   no time to buy any
thing to bring along to eat   just beck
ett   i got on the bus only one other
passenger an old lady   uneventful
through the tunnel the view of the sky
line   down the turnpike through new
jersey   some   other   city   newark

He leaveth the City,
his bane & his home.
Coleridge, Lowry,
can we join hands?

Delaware Water Gap,
  wide
river, fruit trees
flowering: summer
  via spring.
Kittatinny Mts.—
sadist counselors, me
a skinny kid, proto-
  wordsworthian:
morning clouds stretch
  & rise sleepy from
  mt. tops.

The terminal with its
corrupt loafers the
City again.

Eccentricity: a trope

maybe patterson one of those
picked up several more passengers
very ugly here the city   the cities
the industry   i wanted not to look at
it   the roadside stands the mechanics
the garages the custard palaces ice
cream hamburgers   bee urgers   fish
and chimps   so i got out beckett and
tried to read   it was lousy reading on
the bus it hurt my eyes   we were get
ting into the country anyway   i put
away beckett   long overdue at the
library what ten cents a day   i stared
at the country it was nice being in the
country again   by the time we got to
scranton at five i was headachey from
hunger   the nasty lunchcounter man
in the scranton terminal from whom i
bought some cigarillos   then on to
ithaca via another bus   sitting in sec
ond seat in front of me a student from
the west indies next to him sits down
this middle-aged lady   she hadn't
been on the last bus nor was he i think
    the moment she sits down she starts
talking and she didn't stop till we ar
rived   the guy hardly said twenty
words the whole trip   three hours or
something like that   she was talking
about her life   she was english   she
had been brought up in oxford she ex
plained how oxford had been very
pretty but then they moved in an auto
factory and then a steel factory to
supply the auto factory   she married
an american or i guess a canadian and
they came to this country   she was
one of those english eccentrics   her
hangup was oxygen   she described

of freedom traumatized
by conformity.

It is true that in New
   York one feels
freer at night:
official reality dozes
   if watchfully;
foghorns, the sense of
   ships to/from
distant ports, one
   breathes more easily.

I had seen large num-
   bers of horses
   in the mountains,
untended in the fields,
   unsaddled,
moving in herds.

the whole story of her life in terms of
getting enough oxygen   once living
in new jersey for example they had
rented a house   she made her hus
band give it up because of the factory
smoke they had to move to new york
new york wasn't so bad because she
said the sea air it was full of oxygen at
night   after she was married she went
to visit her in-laws somewhere in the
backwoods of canada they were men
nonites   they didn't want their son to
marry outside their religion   they
were very strict   a sect   but they
were very nice to her she said   only
they put her into a room into which
coal gas from the furnace escaped
every night she would get sick   and
apparently in fact according to her
coal gas can be lethal   so there she
was getting sicker and sicker and
finally one day her husband's youngest
sister came in and let slip something
about the coal gas that it was escaping
into the room and when she asked why
she hadn't been told about this the girl
said her parents told her that if it was
god's will to take her then he would
take her and the matter was really out
of their hands   she thought that was
pretty cruel   her search for oxygen
was taking her up to ithaca   her hus
band who had taught english and was
now in the college administration busi
ness was i think administrating in new
york but she had taken it upon herself
to come to ithaca and see if they
couldn't both get jobs working for the
university   and she kept asking the

There are times I
feel I'm suffocating
my breath comes shal-
low panting I think
of a man I heard of
dying with a heart
attack gasping I
can't breathe I
can't breathe.
There's nothing wrong
with my heart.

Like Odysseus 10 years.

student about ithaca whether it was
big whether it had much industry in
short   whether or not there was
enough oxygen   at first i thought this
lady was a real nut   naturally she be
lieved in reincarnation   her husband
she said was a very nice man but he
was very cranky and nasty and he
couldn't get along with people and she
thought perhaps he would learn that in
his next life   she was also a socialist
    a proselytizing socialist   after a
while it struck me though that her
ideas after all weren't so insane   that
they were pretty humane   what was
wrong with a proselytizing socialist
reincarnation   well that's harmless
and after all she had a point about
oxygen   in a way i feel and i would
come to feel more after being in ithaca
that my life too all our lives was a
struggle for sufficient oxygen   ithaca
    i hope i'm saying all i want to say
    katz wasn't home   i called   his
wife answered   seemed glad to hear
from me   i walked over just long
enough to drop my bags   nice girl
pretty too   up to the campus   i took
a cab   no other way of getting up the
hill this time of night   about nine
no buses   incredible   i was walking
in a dream   in memory rather   noth
ing was real because everything was
exactly the same   it wasn't real be
cause it was all in my mind   johnny's
big red grill the royal palm across the
street still there   i felt as if i could put
my hand right through them   they
weren't there   they were in my head

Real means locating
the present in terms
  of the past
locating the self
in terms of the
  present.
Wordsworth, Proust.

and the food in johnny's as bad as
ever   things began to settle into place
    present and past made connections
located one another so to speak   ad
amov was there in johnny's   walked
in a little after me   i had seen him
the week before with mutual friends
sitting next to the stage in a kitchen
while he lectured about the modern
french theater and two hundred al
gerians drowned in the seine by the
french police   things were becoming
real again   i walked over the gorge
onto campus   again the feeling of
walking through memory   the feeling
that everything was in my head   but
then the big new modern library
again things began to fall into place
the past vis-à-vis the present   i looked
at the night view the lights in the val
ley a few glimmering lights in the hill
opposite   distant   the students going
from dormitory to library across the
big campus   the girls i was interested
in mostly   some nice-looking ones
a different genre from the city   a dif
ferent genre from other colleges too
they looked like they lived in the coun
try   they looked like they lived in
a country club   healthy sunburned
lithe   the library tower more impres
sive than i remembered   more beauti
ful even perhaps   the discovery that
the old library was not gothic but
romanesque   i hadn't known the dif
ference before   i got katz out of his
carrel in the new library very luxe
very air-conditioned   sculpture by
lipschitz   katz glad to see me   so it

seemed   that cheered me up   hard
to contact katz   with words   do bet
ter with a slap on the shoulder
telling a story maybe a joke   not
evasive but oblique   wednesday   for
the first time in months it seems i get
up as early as eight thirty   not only
up but wide-awake   the outside is
flooded with sunlight the air totally
different from new york   fresh   race
into the bathroom shave not quite in
time to catch katz   linger a bit over
coffee then take a bus up   the campus
in the daytime   quite different
more real   clarity   again the girls
not quite so dazzling as last night   be
ginning to get used to them   still
quite a few pretty ones   coffee in the
straight and one of those great glazed
doughnuts they don't make them like
that anywhere else why   as usual as
always coffee in the straight in the
morning a laxative effect   up to the
john   back out to the terrace   just
sitting   the view of the valley   i
think of wordsworth   hard to get in
touch with people looking for an apart
ment   i call from the straight go back
to the terrace sit there incredible sun
light blue sky back to the phones
first few apartments very discouraging
    rickety old wooden places with
creepy landladies looking at every
body as they go up and down the stairs
    cramped quarters   firetraps   too
much money   discouraging   car ads
look hopeful though maybe i'll be able
to get a car here too   the students are
different   the good students i mean
about five percent of them maybe   as

usual apart from the fraternities they
cluster in the straight in johnny's in
apartments   now the girls are allowed
to stay out overnight stay in the apart
ments   seniors even some of them
can live out   poetry fiction published
in the student magazine that ten years
ago would have gotten you thrown out
just like that   thing about a girl mas
turbating in front of a creative-writing
class on the teacher's desk with the
teacher's grade book published in the
magazine katz told me about it and
me ten years ago a national issue a
huge fuss between administration and
the arts just because i wrote birdshit in
a story   not only that   though   the
spirit of berkeley   demonstrations
vietnam santo domingo pacifists anti-
rotc   rotc   it really does me good to
see students demonstrating against
rotc   poor marty   marching up and
down in barton hall hour after hour
always some new violation   did he
ever catch up on the penalty hours he
had to march in barton hall   dis
gusting   imagine going to college to
march with a rifle in barton hall
alone back and forth   they even have
trouble finding things to demonstrate
against it seems   *tant mieux*   the big
thing a demonstration the other day in
barton hall at the presidential review
of rotc at which about 80 demonstra
tors sat down on the floor so they
couldn't march   against them the
damn fraternities mobilized twenty-
five-hundred students apparently in a
murderous mood carrying signs kill
kill kill drop the bomb etc   somewhat

anti-semitic too   good old fraternities
    violence prevented only by the cam
pus patrol protecting the demonstra
tors   dick gregory was coming up to
give a speech there were demonstra
tions there too   people demonstrating
for dick gregory against dick gregory
and then a whole sorority full of nice
girls demonstrating against the anti-
gregory demonstrators   an unusual
sorority withdrew from the national
that was complaining they took in too
many negroes and no doubt jews too
    now one wonders why don't they
dissolve the sorority and just become
people   place shown to me by a law
school student a creepy guy   vaguely
in favor of the demonstrations but he
told me they were just creating more
enemies   he wanted everybody to
be nice and well-behaved   nobody
should cause trouble seemed to be the
idea   obviously worried that some
how he might get involved there might
be repercussions   of course he had
liberal ideas but   he didn't want his
career to get messed up by things
changing too much   no chaos
couldn't afford that   a crummy place
anyway   later on standing in front of
the straight waiting for a guy to pick
me up in a car to look at another car
that he had somewhere on the out
skirts   i was watching somebody
making a speech   some undergradu
ate guitar group singing civil-rights
songs trying to get people to the dick
gregory thing   which in turn was a
benefit for some harlem project or for
some southern project i don't remem

ber which   drive out with a new
yorky type   shows me his car   total
wreck   wants 150 for it   every time
you get near the thing you tear your
clothes the body was in such bad
shape   couldn't try it out because he
didn't have plates i didn't have time
gave me advice on apartments   bar
gain he said bargain them down they
have to get rid of them cheap for the
summer   i asked him then if he'd
take 125 for the car   he guessed he
would   i never saw him again   he
told me he goes swimming in the reser
voir where i swam with ***** at dusk
and saw a loon   that night at katz's
his kids clambering all over him like
one of his stories   i couldn't imagine
katz with three kids i'd never seen him
with his kids   what would he be like
   well there it was   it was like katz
with three kids   nice to see   obvi
ously had an empathy with children
his own anyway   the younger one
coos when he talks   they're three
boys   that afternoon late after a long
exhausting search up and down the
famous hill i found something i
thought i might like   collegetown's
ugly one apartment house   not really
an apartment house although there
are enough apartments in it   but not
really an apartment house by new
york standards four floors made of
white concrete apartment on the first
floor pretty cheap cheaper than i ex
pected   memories connected with
that house   especially this one   in
the crescent drive in the front meeting
***** i was in front of the house she

was at one end of the drive a white
sweater as i remember running to
wards me must have been glad to see
me i guess she liked me i remember as
she ran how her breasts bounced her
big silky breasts silky nipples   the
french influence no doubt as i now
realized the bouncing a french bras
siere   all through collegetown memo
ries   all the places still there
******'s apartment downstairs how
much smaller i was then   how little
   how little i knew   how much big
ger she was than me   and of course i
knew it which was why i was afraid of
her   as indeed there was good reason
to be   and ****'s old place   the site
so to speak of my first mistress my first
   real sex if not exactly my first fuck
   **** sneaking out at night to snip
her neighbor's giant tulips and bring
them to me   katz's wife makes spice
bread all her own bread only white
bread in packages in ithaca   and
sourbread too   and chala for the
weekend   late that night i close the
deal on the apartment   the thing that
really won me over   and despite not
because of the memories   the fact
that the gorge so close   i saw a beauti
ful bird there   red beak   red head
i walked down along a path   over
looking falls rapids pools trees above
   the gorges here and there still quite
primeval   and at the top above the
falls tennis courts in the middle of the
woods   i imagine myself walking
through the gorge up to the courts
playing a while back into the gorge to

Looking back with
some urgency to find
a place to write
Is this the gorge
where Bogotay
died the year
after I left I
find no room &
then discover that
p. 12 I missed in
pagination was
that your ghost
Joe then let this
space be a memorial
death is white a
blank a young man's
death a page unwritten
therefore a propos
besides you were no
architect never even
finished that but a
tinkerer over jobs
undone like your car
your brother I think
finished it it turned
up like a ghost in
Cambridge it was the
tinkering you liked
you never meant to
finish life why else
were you shooting
rapids in a flood
damn fool tinkering
as you would say you
built a boat in your
bedroom I helped you
hoist it out &
left it on the lawn
en route to L.A.
where we sped around
on the crazy carcass
of your unfinished car.

There seems to be an
error of chronology
here: I think this
happened the night
before. That too
has its value—to
capture the present
with the collusion
of the past. Let
it stand.

Or was my lust still
weak, a mere tickling
of the surface, a
thing of the eye?
A queer painter once
told me that sight is
the most sensual
of the senses: I
asked him, What
about touch?

From Wordsworth one

cool off in a pool and back to the
house   so i take the apartment   i
pick up steve in his carrel   at the
same moment i'm meeting him i raise
my hand in greeting he raises his hand
but in greeting someone behind me
next to me a nice-looking young girl
    a senior but she looks a lot younger
than that   i say why don't you come
along with us   we all go for a beer
i was coming on strong   girl obvi
ously impressed   after a while in
johnny's nothing to say   all the ten
sion suddenly getting expressed   be
ing here breaking through the memory
barrier the effort of finding a place the
fact of finding it the displacement
from new york   not much left to be
charming   to a girl for whom in any
case my desire would be merely carnal
    if that   not much for me there
by this time i'm absolutely sick of
cornell   the scenery is beautiful   the
gorges wonderful   that's it   every
thing else depresses me   especially all
the deja views   i feel trapped here
the students make me feel claustro
phobic   i wish i were back in new
york   still at every table in johnny's
    the talk about the demonstration in
barton hall   the booing of Johnson's
foreign policy spokesman   that's en
couraging that makes me feel good
making him show his true colors who
has flown the flag of liberalism for
how long twenty or thirty years   just
another pricky billionaire   talking
too low too slow   next day   thurs
day   up every morning at nine this is
fantastic   i don't even get tired oh i
get tired but i recuperate   more and

passes inevitably
to Lawrence: from
health of habitat to
health of the animal
itself.

more energy   of course i know this
that activity generates energy   torpor
    just dissipates it   i know it and yet
in new york of course i forget it or if
not forget it just know it incapable of
doing anything about it   the sunlight
the view of the valley   still another
stage looking at the students   that is
first i was dazzled by the girls then
quite sick of them   now i begin to
single different ones out   my lusts are
scattered all across the campus   a
beautiful indian girl i keep seeing
a graduate student katz tells me
daughter of some important indian
government person   incredibly expen
sive clothing she wears   saris   one
of the few indian girls i've ever found
attractive   after a few days she gets
to know me by sight   she's interested
    a hard look in the eyes she gives me
mysterious dark brown eyes   another
girl an older one   must be some
body's wife eating alone in johnny's
    not far from my table   looking at
me out of the corner of her eye   this
one really good-looking   an actress
face   elegant figure   i could go over
and ask her if she wants to have a
drink or if i could join her   no doubt
she wants me to   would she say no
so what   if i handled it right she'd
say yes   and yet   i'm not really on
the make here   it interests me   but
it doesn't interest me really   she
leaves   i cheer up on the terrace i
look at more cars   i begin to cancel
out ads in the papers   i get it down
to a choice between a few   i'm be
ginning to feel better and better   i
think it's the oxygen really   i'm

finally getting enough oxygen   here
away from new york   that afternoon
i see a ford that looks good   but there
are a few other cars i want to check
at some point or other i meet the
leader of the student demonstrations
briefly   obviously a new york jew
he's supposed to be all sensibility   the
guy with the charisma   i can see that
in his face   i wonder how conscious
is he   how much does it matter that
he's the center of things   how much
is he interested in power at heart
how much is he interested in the in
evitable fringe vulgarities of such a
position   how much is he like or un
like myself when ten years ago i was
briefly a campus hero of sorts and
girls would come up to me as i would
walk across campus and my immedi
ate reflex was to be as nasty as possi
ble   for which i always kicked myself
afterwards   because some of them
were pretty and one i remember
throwing   herself   away   on   some
shmuck   who i had seen around a
lot   and lusted after   i was uncertain
about him the charismatic guy   ex
tremely difficult to get through that
ten years and see what things are re
ally like   though here i have a dou
ble view   my paranoia for example
ten years ago with regard to frater
nity types   the real americans   the
square-jawed arrogant types   the
blond girls with money and pedigree
some where behind them   my para
noia of these types which after leaving
i had thought stupid   now i see was
not only absolutely justified but in fact

i have it again   of these students
from whom i have nothing at the mo
ment at all to fear but who i do fear
and i know now as i knew then in
stinctively   with good reason   hard
to get through that ten years   what
would i have thought of that girl i met
the other day   not merely that there
was no contact nothing there for me
but possibly that she was an idiot even

The chaos of my mind.

despite her sharpness her intelli
gence   the fact that she took all the
right positions   maybe   in fact no
doubt and this is a comfort   if i got
to know her i think i would think the
same thing of her now as one way or
another i would have thought of her
then   one sees the same types   one
has the impulse to tap them on the
shoulder and call them by the same
names   one is convinced they would
answer to them   and yet there is this
difference   the spirit the demonstra
tions   the rebellion   much healthier
that night at dinner i decide which
car to buy   i feel that i'm somewhat
out of contact with my host and host
ess my mind is always on other things
business   the cars   the apartments
is this what it's like to be a business
man   i call lynn i had called her be
fore   last night to tell her i got an
apartment   she'll wire me money for
the car   at the end of dinner i decide
which car to get   despite the suspi
cious radiator the ford   when was it
that i began to feel good   essentially
i think it was when i woke up the first
morning at eight thirty   the sunlight
outside the oxygen   still the tension

of the car but that's almost over
next morning i close the deal   by then
i'm exhausted   this is friday   i go to
all the necessary offices do all the nec
essary things   i'm really knocked out
    i pick up the car put the plate on
say goodbye   go to a gas station get
some gas open the hood   the radiator
that had supposedly just been fixed
was spurting a steady stream of water
    a regular geyser   when was it i
started feeling so good   was it during
the walk in the gorge i think so   or
was it the continual buzz among the
students in collegetown in the straight
the enclave of intellectuals or bohe
mians or whatever they were was it
that   sitting on the terrace the other
day waiting to get in touch with some
one with a car   a group of students
couldn't quite figure out the boys
their haircuts may be the beatle influ
ence   obviously campus intellectuals
    dungarees and so on   only their
style of dress their style in general had
a kind of chic to it   the boys looked
sort of pretty   i tried to place them
among people i had known ten years
ago   these types were different   they
would have been dirtier   they would
have been less self-conscious or self-
conscious in a different way   what
would i have thought of these people
then   i couldn't quite make them out
    the girls though one of them a
blond not bad-looking   i could place
her all right   the blond one   cud
dling up to her pretty boyfriend   es
caped from a sorority   brains enough
to know that the more interesting peo

ple didn't have anything to do with
fraternity sorority life   essentially not
very different from her ex-sorority sis
ters   in five years you would hardly
know the difference   i knew girls like
that   the other was different   nice-
looking girl   baby face sexy body
very young   but whereas the others
seemed to be playacting she seemed
to be uninterested in acting any par
ticular role   they were talking about
the demonstrations in barton hall
she had been one of the sittees   her
case had come up before some disci
plinary board   apparently as she ex
plained it they were reprimanded
they considered this a light sentence
    two students looking up   the sky
very blue   wispy clouds   jet bomber
refueling in midair   way up   tiny
white outlines against blue   vapor
trail   you could see them one plane
flying slightly behind the other   now
i'm lying on the bed   in full view of
the full-length mirror   closed off here
    lynn on the phone in the other
room   planes overhead   below   un
der the bomber   the issue   stop the
war in viet nam   santo domingo
rotc   one's sense of the enor
mous privilege of the students here
a country club   grownups would pay
large sums of money to come here sit
on the terrace drinking beer   a sense
of awe   at the lightness with which i
held this privilege when i was here
ready to throw it away so easily   i
was quite aghast at this   suppose i
had done so   in fact i had done so
    and was saved only by a quirk of

faculty administration politics   the
ten years' difference   obviously i
would do the same thing again   they
had been reprimanded she was explain
ing carefully   she sympathized with
the dean in charge   he wasn't bad
he had to do his job he was conserva
tive but he was sympathetic she could
understand his position   the students
in front of the straight talking the
other day   there was a petition they
were getting a lot of signatures against
the demonstrations   two white guys
were telling a black girl   there are
quite a few more blacks here now
a negro in the john the other day   i
typed him as one of the athletes   still
the kind of negro there because he
could play football or was good at
track   singing of all things old man
river in the john   very palsy walsy
with a negro porter cleaning things
up there as if they really had some
thing in common   and i guess they
did but this girl one of the new types
apparently there for no reason but
that she was smart   explaining that
it would do no good to get up a coun
terpetition because in any case they
were the minority   taking advantage
a little of being able to be authorita
tive because she was black   knew
i was listening too showing off for me
i could see that   the bomber refuel
ing overhead   a kid taking the line
that perhaps it would be better not to
irritate people any further at the mo
ment   baby face explaining carefully
and patiently why this was no good
it was a doubt raised not out of inter

est in the issue but out of a desire to
be part of this group which apparently
had some prestige   i would not have
been so patient i would have ignored
the question totally   i didn't like the
boys   they were too pretty   there
was a kind of chic involved   there
was a false note it wasn't merely the
issue   a kid came over he could have
been in tep   the jewish fraternity   he
probably wasn't but he was coming on
like a fraternity boy singing whatever
he had to say really coming on   the
other boys the pretty ones joined in
took up this tone   after a while the
girl got up without saying anything
and walked away looking bored   the
pseudofraternity type yelled after her
you just don't like us because we're
jewish still that issue   later on i found
out that she too was jewish   she had
said that they were giggling in the
dean's office because all the demon
strators turned out to have jewish
names and they were all from brook
lyn or the bronx   the mechanic said
he could solder the radiator   two dol
lars or so   i believe it turned out to
be four   which is usually what two
dollars or so means in the mouth of a
mechanic   he was an old type very
rustic robert frost would have liked
him   i had to have the emergency-
brake cable tightened   i came back
an hour later he had finished soldering
the radiator just finishing the emer
gency brake i said how are the rest of
the brakes   apparently in fixing up
the emergency they had discovered
that the brakes were no good at all

dangerous in fact   sixty bucks   the
car was 150   i had felt bad when i
tried to bargain the guy down to 125

he was such a nice guy   all the peo
ple with used cars up there for sale
were very nice   except the first car i
looked at the new york guy   who
ended up giving me advice on bargain
ing and who was obviously trying to
get rid of a wreck   but the natives
were very nice   a middle-aged lady
out of small town usa very respectable
very helpful very honest   no doubt
a couple of kids from maybe pennsyl
vania with a morris minor they bought
from an english professor at swarth
more   the guy i bought my car from
nicest of all   everybody with a good
reason for selling the car just got a
new one couldn't pass it up and so on

he'd put a lot of money into that
car he said he was only selling it that
cheap because well in effect that was
all he could get for it   could it be that
these nice people were cheats in their
nice way   isn't just that the great
american hypocrisy   maybe   maybe
not   anyway there i was with a sixty-
dollar brake job on my hands   and
god knows what else   this rustic type
standing there looking at the car and
saying yep the gutless fifty-eight don't
know why ford ever made that car   i
should have felt worse   but i knew
the routine so well   i kept saying to
myself something like it's all part of
the fun of owning a car   an essen
tially american experience buying a
used car mechanics with their ambig
uous smiles of concern the clap on the

shoulder from the buyer as you drive
off the feeling of never knowing and
never being able to know whether you
were cheated or whether he didn't
know either   or whether it was just
that he didn't want to know   i should
have felt worse   but it wasn't only
that i knew the routine   it was the
oxygen   the oxygen was buoying me
up   i drove around i found a cheaper
place   a forty-dollar estimate made
an appointment to bring the car back
that night   went back to katz's ex
hausted   i still felt good   i was feel
ing better and better   it was the oxy
gen the trees the sunlight the students
with their demonstrations katz's kids
clambering over him like one of his
stories his wife making bread her shy
ness   after dinner we went up to a
campus place a student place over
looking the lake the falls one of the
falls   in this place a girl with huge
boobs shorts and a cap pistol looking
disheveled   walking around with her
enormous breasts shooting off her cap
pistol   a mathematician with another
cap pistol must be some kind of fad
    said he was drunk   we went out
side we were going to a party   the
mathematician not only had a cap pis
tol but in his car he also had a whip
    a bullwhip   he showed us how he
snapped the bullwhip and fired the pis
tol at the same time   the impression
was supposed to be that was the way
he dealt with women i believe   we
went to the party an architects' party
always a lively bunch   katz knew a
lot of people there   i found i really

Out of place, even
ten years ago I
felt too stupid—
the F. Scott Fitz-
    gerald scene:
magic parties, dashing
    girls.

This, of course, is
inexcusably gross—
it is a way in which
I am inexcusably gross.

couldn't face it i had something to
drink the people were doing the twist
or whatever version it is now   lively
    lots of nice-looking girls   there
was the girl on the terrace baby face
    was it her yes   in a sensational
dress   showing the exaggerated s of
her figure   i asked her where the
drinks were she told me i wanted to
say more   i felt too stupid   i would
have liked to have gotten to know her
    i was curious   i had said one night
at dinner that i heard this student talk
ing in this impressively clearheaded
way and i wondered if there were stu
dents who at that age she looked like
a freshman   when i was here who
could have been that clearheaded at
that age   i went over to katz that's
the girl i was talking about i said
    more punch appeared i drank two
or three glasses   some girl attached
herself to me   not very pretty   a
familiar type   brooklyn intellectual
must have known hundreds like her
    who i also didn't like   i got mildly
rude   she went away for a while
and then came back   katz seemed
to know all the pretty girls at the
party   i spotted him at the other
side of the room   talking to my
clinging intellectual acquaintance and
the clearheaded girl   i went over
the liquor luckily was getting to me
    i barged into the middle of the con
versation explaining that i could never
be one of the cool faculty types like
katz because i couldn't get myself to
act stupid enough unless i got drunk
that wasn't a nice thing to say   no

body minded   the clearheaded girl
was very drunk   she knew she was
very drunk   she was having fun be
ing very drunk   this time i got into
a conversation with her   a three-way
conversation me her and the plain girl
   she's wearing my earrings i'm wear
ing hers which do you like better   it
was turning into a competitive thing
katz had disappeared   i was enjoying
myself   i like yours better i said to
the pretty girl and pointed out how
that was a two-way compliment and
felt myself very suave   i was enjoying
myself   the girls were friends   each
was trying to get me away from the
other   i overplayed it   the pretty girl
got bored again as she had on the
terrace and there i was again left with
that brooklyn intellectual   those hun
dreds of brooklyn intellectual girls
i got away somehow   i bumped into
the pretty girl again   she told me she
was very drunk   i asked her for a
cigarette she said it was her last cigar
ette and said with me that's really a
sign of affection   she was coming on
   she wasn't making any secrets about
it either   i said when do you have to
get back twelve thirty she said she was
a sophomore   she could have stayed
out all night if she had signed out
i asked her whether she was going
back with anyone she said no i said
why don't you go home with me she
said okay she said goodbye to her
friend i found katz i told him i'm dis
appearing i'd only been at the party
twenty minutes   i think   we got out
side she told me how high she was she

wasn't that high quite really   but she
was pretty high   we walked down the
street   i held her hand   we got to a
gorge   i put my arm around her
there was a path down into the gorge
it was a warm night   i led her down
    i kissed her   i liked the way she
kissed me   after a while i put my
hands under her dress   i unzipped the
top she made no objections to any
thing   made it clear that she liked it
    she had a wonderful ass   of a type
    the big type   which she said she
knew some people didn't like i told
her i did   but one hoped that it
wouldn't betray her in the future by
getting too big   i had found an
apartment i had found a car   and
now i'd found finally a coed whose ass
i not only admired walking across
campus but which i could also squeeze

Crude! (But true.)

    i felt my trip was a success   i don't
think i even wanted anything else very
much   though i wanted to fuck her
on the spot   on the other hand i knew
she'd been in trouble because of the
demonstrations i knew she had to get

Not carnal but psycho-
logical.

back soon   what i really wanted she
had already given me   she kept ex
plaining how she didn't do this kind
of thing   find a man and practically
jump into bed with him   we were
now lying down on the path   or al
most lying down   on a broad step
shored up in the slope by a split log
    i wasn't sure that we couldn't be
seen from the road   certainly at any
minute somebody could have walked
up or down the path   i really didn't
give a shit   neither did she   i had

her pants down i was playing with
her vagina every now and then she
stopped and said that she didn't usu
ally do this kind of thing that she
shouldn't be doing it and then she
did it with a vengeance she half
suggested that she better get back to
the dorm because she'd be late i
agreed my double view and anyway
it wasn't the sex so much i was after i
knew it even at the moment it was
the gesture that kind of contact with
a girl again and a little ego thrown
in too she said we better hitchhike
back we got a ride right away some
student taking his girl back to the
dorm the backseat conversation
on which the two in front were eagerly
eavesdropping was pretty interesting
  i can't blame them for eavesdrop
ping how old are you thirty-two
i can't believe it i'm only nineteen
you're much too old for me you al
ready have grey hair i pointed out
that i had grey hair when i was twenty-
one but thirty-two she said what
would my parents think i shrugged
  i didn't give a shit what her parents
would think you're much too old for
me she insisted i'd giggle maybe
i'd be giggling too i said she hadn't
done much giggling so far i told her
in the gorge when she suddenly looked
up and said say you aren't married or
something are you i said do you care
she said a friend of mine was going
out with a married man it was very
bad she didn't believe in that kind of
thing so naturally i said no there's
a window where girls can jump out

My double view,
here merged through her
in a single view,
neither one nor the
    other,
past and present
each defining each
finally finding balance.

Not grey hair—grey
    hairs.

She'd told me she's
    a bitch.
Girls that age always
    think they're bitches.
Was this her attempt
    to be a bitch?

in the dormitory   there always had
been   there was ten years ago   i
mildly tried to get her to jump out and
come back after she went in   not too
hard though i didn't want to get her
fucked up   it would have been worth
it perhaps if i were really available   it
would have been worth it   if i were
really available   and there was some
thing else too   she was a smart girl
and above all she was on my side   i
could easily have imagined her as a
friend   had she been a sorority girl it
would have brought out all my sadistic
impulses and those can be fun too

I speak of betrayal,
though of course I was
already proceeding under
the responsibility of
the lie I had chosen
to tell.

but you don't betray people on your
own side   next day i met her after
class   i had nothing in mind   i had
neglected to buy contraceptives i
didn't have a place to stay with her
and i cursed myself for this as i waited
for her but it was really a question of
not wanting to impose my volition on
what would happen   she looked good

My volition: it must
not be something I was
plotting but something
that was happening to
me, that found its own
logic. That was essen-
tial.

she looked good because she looked
like exactly what she was   she was
dressed as a coed   sweater skirt
god they wear short skirts she had nice
thighs   we drove away from the col
lege   i tried to get the lake road but
missed and we went into the hills
above the lake   we didn't talk very
much   i had nothing in mind   i had
to tell her i was married   i drove off
onto a country road we stopped in a
wood i pulled over onto the shoulder
we talked for a few minutes she said
there's a stream down there i hadn't
noticed it   there was a small gully in
the woods and a really lovely little

stream   we went through what
looked a lot like poison ivy she was
wearing sandals and a short skirt and
a sleeveless kind of sweater   i hoped
it wasn't poison ivy   soon as we got
down there we sat on a log over the
stream i put my arm around her that
was it   after a while i had her against
a tree trunk she was standing up
squirming   i think her passion really
wasn't controllable   obviously i could
do anything i wanted with her   i
made her take her pants off i undid
her brassiere i took my cock out it was
huge   i got it between her thighs i

I felt myself slither-   rubbed against her pussy a little and
ing hotly within a con-   put it in   she warned me she was at a
fusion of blind membranes.   fertile period i took it out and con
What right had I to re-   tented myself with rubbing it against
main so conscious with-   her pussy   i put it in now and then
in her urgency, probing   she was squirming like mad   it was
her for private sol-   a nice moment   i thought i would just
utions?   come between her thighs   it didn't
                               really matter   i wanted to lie down
                               with her i took her away from the tree
                                  then i saw when she had a moment
                               to cool off that she was really worried
                               about what she was about to do   i
                               didn't care if it went any further we
                               stopped   she wasn't a crude girl   i
                               wanted it to be clear not only to her
                               but mostly to myself that it wasn't just
                               a question of a piece of ass not that
                               there's anything wrong with a piece of
                               ass but   for the first time i clearly
(I don't think this is true.) knew that it never had been for me
                               ever purely a question of a piece of ass
                               with girls   why then should i make
                               myself feel bad   distort myself into
                               an ugly shape   we went back to the

car we talked a while she talked
about her family she was from the
bronx it turns out despite the way
she looked   which was like a baby
faced girl from say st louis maybe
we had quite similar backgrounds she
was hung up by the same problems
that i had been hung up with   faced
with the problem of what does a
young girl do with her freedom who
doesn't feel in sympathy with ameri
can life   girls at that age are much
freer than men who are concerned
with their careers   the good girls are
concerned with their freedom with
how they can retain themselves   the
girls at that point outnumber the men
   see henry james   and they run the
same risks as jamesian heroines too
and usually they lose out   we talked
about that   it was time to go back
all the time i knew i had to tell her
that i was married   i could have not
told her   she would never see me
again   and i told katz not to tell her
   and again if she were a sorority
girl i wouldn't have told her   but i
couldn't bring myself to do it   i had
intended to tell her as soon as we
stopped the car before   then we went
outside   finally on the road into ith
aca i pulled over on the shoulder and
came out with it   she said i wish you
had told me before that was all   she
wasn't the cryey type   but she looked
like she'd been hit in the face   turned
a little red   she said she believed in
fidelity   i explained what i believed
about it   she said she could under
stand that all right   i tried to pene

She had said I turned
her on. I turned her
on. Now I was turning
her off.

He has a good body, she
said of a boyfriend.
The comedy of my fum-
bling complications blind
to the simplicities of
her lust.

This referral of her
own experience to her
parents: she was per-
haps still a little
babyish—she had said
she was still a little
babyish.

trate ten years   what was she really
like   who was she from the point of
view of myself ten years ago   and
who was she from my point of view
now   she didn't believe in being neu
rotic times had changed   this year
she was neurotic the sophomore year
is always the year   now she accepted
her hang-ups   all the girls i used to
know aside from the european ones
cultivated their neuroses   she said
that was still a style   yet in this seg
ment of this generation things were
much healthier thank god   well i
wish her luck   i decided to give her
adek's address in paris since she was
going to europe next year   people on
the same side have to help one another
out   like antonello and his circuit of
amici from naples to norway   i
started talking about my own ideas as
we drove into ithaca   what it did for
me to be in the country again how i
liked wordsworth   but from that
point on everything i said felt a little
hollow   and she was only half lis
tening   it dawned on me that she was
really sad   i don't know what she had
expected   she was the kind of girl
who didn't expect things too much but
just let them happen   and they hadn't
happened the way she had figured
she really must have contemplated
some extended relation she kept won
dering what would her parents think
of her going out with a thirty-two-year
old   when i told her i was married
she said i guess then that i won't see
you any more   of course i had known
that anyway   she said she had no

Finding someone to
whom I could react
both as what I was then
and what I am now:
unity of experience =
reality of self.

regrets she said she was glad of the
whole thing anyway   maybe   she
probably was in a way but she was
obviously pretty knocked out and was
acting like somebody who had been
punched in the stomach   even though
she may not have known it herself   i
had wanted to do something for her
and i felt that i'd fucked up   i thought
of lynn and i thought that i wasn't
capable of doing anybody any good
at all   but i did give her adek's ad
dress   without getting anything to eat
i started back for new york   i knew
even then that i could have stayed
another night that i could have seen
her that night that i could have rented
a motel talked her into signing out and
spent the night with her   i didn't do
it because i had gotten all i could have
reasonably not reasonably but unrea
sonably all i could have wildly hoped
for already   the question now was
would the car make it to new york
the car worked fine   outside ithaca i
stopped to get something to eat
picked some flowers for lynn   i was
driving through rain all the way
through the mountains through fog
through clouds really   with the sun
breaking through now and then very
beautiful   following the same route i
had taken so many times driving back
and forth from cornell some of the old
places were still there   the roads were
better though   when i knew the car
was going to be ok   and i was about
two thirds of the way to new york i
started being able to pick up new york
stations i got some good music   i

A particular & recur-
ring experience the
sum of which is: feel-
ing keenly in harmony
with my own impulses &
anarchically indepen-
dent of constrictions
which deaden them—
an experience essen-
tial to the psychology
of freedom.

started singing along with the radio
i felt wonderful in fact the last time i
felt just this way was when i finally
left cornell   both times singing like a
maniac   both times total enjoyment
of driving a big american car on a
smooth american highway with jazzy
american music   alone in the car
the mountains later darkness   other
car lights   that was all   and the
theme song was happy days are here
again da-da-da da-da good cheer
again da-da-da da-da da-da da-da
happy days are here again   and that
was it   because i was absolutely re
incarnated   i had gotten all the oxy
gen i needed   and i was passing into
another life   a life in which i incor
porated all the things i'd known in
past lives but had forgotten   and
added them to all the new things i had
learned   i had been driving for five
or six hours i wasn't tired   i was full
of energy   i wanted to get back and
show lynn the car   lynn looked at me
as if i looked different   and she told
me i looked different   and i was dif
ferent   what had happened was that
i had broken out of my reality into
another and better one   which in
cluded the former   but refreshed it as
well   so in a way i was coming back
a stranger and i knew it   i couldn't
help myself for trying to bring her into
my reality she couldn't help herself for
not being in it   i suppose it was in
evitable that there was a conflict   i
began to feel miserable   there was
nothing i could do about it   again i
had the feeling that i couldn't do any

thing good for anybody   but i knew
as certainly as i ever know anything
that i had hold of myself had hold of
my experience no had hold of a level
of experience   that i mustn't ever lose

This gloss: N.Y.'s
compulsive marginalia.

sight of again   that i had to somehow
hold on to it   that it was very impor
tant   that it was important not only
to me but for lynn and not only for
lynn   but for everyone i knew   and
not only for people i knew but for
myself in public aspects that is as a
teacher but most importantly   as a
writer   so i decided that in the morn
ing i'd better get it all down as quick
as i could while it was alive and i did
i hope am doing it because   what else

What else a lot of
things but among

is writing for

them to capture those moments in their crudeness duplicity blind
egoism those moments to which de
spite these things we return from
which we begin again toward which
we continually recuperate.

THE DEATH OF THE NOVEL

Fiction constitutes a way of looking at the world. Therefore I will begin by considering how the world looks in what I think we may now begin to call the contemporary post-realistic novel. Realistic fiction presupposed chronological time as the medium of a plotted narrative, an irreducible individual psyche as the subject of its characterization, and, above all, the ultimate, concrete reality of things as the object and rationale of its description. In the world of post-realism, however, all of these absolutes have become absolutely problematic.

The contemporary writer—the writer who is acutely in touch with the life of which he is part—is forced to start from scratch: Reality doesn't exist, time doesn't exist, personality doesn't exist. God was the omniscient author, but he died; now no one knows the plot, and since our reality lacks the sanction of a creator, there's no guarantee as to the authenticity of the received version. Time is reduced to presence, the content of a series of discontinuous moments. Time is no longer purposive, and so there is no destiny, only chance. Reality is, simply, our experience, and objectivity is, of course, an illusion. Personality, after passing through a phase of awkward self-consciousness, has become, quite minimally, a mere locus for our experience. In view of these annihilations, it should be no surprise that literature, also, does not exist—how could it? There is only reading and writing, which are things we do, like eating and making love, to pass the time, ways of maintaining a considered boredom in face of the abyss.

Not to mention a series of overwhelming social dislocations.

I walked into the cafeteria. I had been hired to teach an ad-

vanced honors seminar on The Death of the Novel. The kids
from my class were sitting around over coffee, listening to rock
'n' roll and reading comic books.

That was the spring, collegetown. Up here on the mountain
the slopes are covered with snow. I've just come in from sledding.
I was lying in the middle of a snowy field on my sled in the sun.
The sky, pale around the sun, was deep burning blue in the north
over the mountains. I could see individual snow crystals glistening
as the sled cut through the powdery surface. A downy woodpecker pecked at some branches near the ground. I stood there
watcing within two feet of him. The day liquefies and flows like
an ongoing improvisation, a fluency fluid as flux. We improvise
our art as we improvise our lives. No hysterical impositions of
meaning.

I was in my apartment on the Lower East Side. My wife was
out, my mistress was tied up with her husband, I was waiting for
my girlfriend to come over. She was fifteen. Meanwhile downstairs, Regis was cooking up a pot of what he called "beef get-
together" for supper, and upstairs on the fifth floor Mr. Duke lay
bloated and purple, dead for a week and beginning to smell. Up
till then the neighbors had thought it was another rat dead in
the wall. I hate chronology, that's what kills us.

Not to mention various overwhelming social dislocations.

> at least four times hit her with
> all his force then thrust his club
> swordlike between her hands into
> her face two more troops came up
> and began dragging the girl we
> could see her face but there was
> no face raw skin and blood her
> eyes had filled with the blood
> pouring down her head she vom-
> ited that too blood

A day of ruined meditation. As I'm about to start work the
contractor who takes care of the house shows up to fix the roof
leak. A beefy heavy man, he stops in front of the snow dolmen
I had set up and before I could tell him to go around it says,
What's this? and with two quick brutal strokes of his shovel
handle shatters it to bits. My snow sculpture, I told him. He

snorts, and tramples across the remains. No escape. The long
dirty finger of my country pokes its way into my life, even here,
ivory tower, white snow, monastic. I drive into town for the
rock salt he says I need to melt the ice off the roof, come back
with a paper.

> Spock and Coffin indicted in anti-
> draft activities

The long dirty finger.

> if convicted the men could receive
> maximum penalties of five years
> in prison and $10,000 fines the
> indictment represents the strong-
> est countermove by the govern-
> ment so far

Will they hit the rest of us? Commitment to civil disobedience,
under the circumstances, an act of health. Changes your life.
Helps define your soul.

> its about time said Representative
> F. Edward Hébert (D., La.)

The long dirty finger.

> pressure mounts for bombing halt
> appeals to Johnson come from
> senators rabbi and Bonn socialists
> administration spokesmen de-
> clined to comment on appeals to
> stop the bombing and would not
> elaborate on the explanation by
> Secretary of State Dean Rusk yes-
> terday that the United States was
> trying to learn whether Hanoi seri-
> ously wanted to enter negotiations
> or was engaged only in a propa-
> ganda move the State Department
> spokesman responded with a
> firm no comment Representative
> L. Mendel Rivers the South Caro-
> lina Democrat who heads the
> House Armed Services Commit-
> tee took the opposite tack assert-

ing his hope that we are not going
to be suckers for North Vietnamese tricks

Moscow the Soviet Union charged
today that United States aircraft
seriously damaged a Soviet mer-
chant vessel while bombing the
North Vietnamese port of Haiphong yesterday

President DeGaulle assured the
Grand Rabbi of France that it was
far from his intention to insult the
Jews when he called them an elite
people sure of itself and domineer-
ing he told the Rabbi that he was
surprised when his phrase was in-
terpreted as being anti-semitic in
character

Prince Sihanouk said if President
Johnson is willing to prevent ag-
gression against our country the
Bowles visit would at least permit
a reduction of tension between the
United States and Cambodia

Senator William Proxmire listed
today the names of 23 defense
contractors among thousands that
he said were wasting hundreds of
millions of dollars through im-
proper use of Defense Department
property I think this is an excellent example of the military-
industrial complex at work with
the victim being the taxpayer

the National Archives made public today the text of the agreement
under which autopsy photographs
and X rays of President Kennedy's
body will be held secret until Oc-
tober 29, 1971

Hoover says reds use black power
there is nothing which the party
would like more than to witness a
continuation of widespread opposition especially non-communist
opposition to the government's
policy in Viet Nam Mr. Hoover
said

The long dirty finger with its obscene transforming touch. The
sun is in, the sky has turned dirty grey. The icicles hang like
snot from

at least four times hit her with
all his force then thrust his club
swordlike between her hands into
her face two more troops came up
and began dragging the girl we
could see her face but there was
no face raw skin and blood her
eyes had filled with the blood
pouring down her head she vom-
ited that too blood

As one icicle said to another, Stay cool, you drip. Or as the
Chinese convert said to the congregation, Let us play.

I sat down at the table next to Betty, who was poring over the
latest Mary Marvel.

Speaking of the death of the novel, I said. When I get nervous
sometimes I get a little pompous. Especially with students. Especially with students who I want to seduce. The kids at the table
smiled at one another indulgently. They liked me. They thought
I was hip. For my age. They knew I wanted to make it with Betty.
They probably wished me luck. Their attitude seemed to be if
that's what he wants, we wish him luck. They knew it didn't
mean that much to Betty. As one of them said to me later, She
makes it with everybody man. Then added thoughtfully, Almost
everybody. Their attitude was that it didn't mean that much
whether I wanted to fuck Betty, or if I didn't want to fuck Betty,
or if in fact I did fuck Betty. That seemed to be pretty much
Betty's attitude too. She was a cheerleader type, one of those
auburn straight-haired round-cheeked dolls right out of a Coca-
Cola ad. As a matter of fact she was elected Miss High School

Coed of South Dakota for 1965. She came to college, did the sorority-fraternity bit for a year, got laid, got pregnant, got married, got aborted, got annulled, spent another year getting A's in all her courses, then gave up. I was just catching up with civilization in those days, she told me. Now I'm caught up. I liked her. She was pretty as apples and bland as Uneeda Biscuits. Her thighs were like white bread. She walked around like she owned it all. She expected men to be gallant to her, and they were. She could cut a girl's heart out with her nail file, and I've seen her do it. She expected everybody to be polite, and give her things, and kiss her ass, and they did, for no better reason that I could see but that she expected them to. But she was generous and had a funny kind of impartiality about her favors, as long as she got whatever it was she wanted. It all would have worked out better if she really knew what it was. She was pretty in the most negotiable way, only she didn't trade on it for all she could get, but only for what she thought she wanted, and she didn't want what she looked like she should have wanted: home, hubby with bow tie, chubby twins, and an inexhaustible supply of Coca-Cola. Still, she was America, and I wanted her. In any case she was my smartest student, and I wanted her the way a teacher always wants his smartest student, especially if she's a nice piece of ass. Not that she ever did any work. I gave her A for her ideas, for her conversation, for her presence maybe, for her pussy, and because getting A's didn't mean a thing to her.

Speaking of the death of the novel, I said. Once comic books imitated fiction. Soon we're going to have fiction like comic books.

She tossed her hair back out of her face. Does it matter? she asked.

Frankly I could never tell when she was high and when she wasn't. She always had that same flat neutral talky manner. Live in the moment, stay cool, keep your balance. It's all a boring game. Nobody wins, so above all don't think man, just keep playing. They were always high on one thing or another most of those kids. It was a strange thing to teach a class to seven or eight different states of consciousness. Kids up, kids going up like rockets and talking a blue streak you couldn't shut them up, kids sitting in the corners of the room sweating and having visions. Even when a kid wasn't on anything you had the feeling he was like down. The straight kids didn't know what was coming off. One would deliver a paper for a half an hour, and at the end some cat would raise his hand and say something very slow and weird, like, Banana pie, and giggle. The only thing that saved that class was that I didn't give a damn what they did, I just made sure I was having a good time. That got them curious. My attitude was, if they got curious and wanted to talk to me about the death of the novel, cool; and if they didn't I was just as happy to sit around and think out loud.

Reality has become a literal chaos. It has escaped our definitions. I'm reading from my notes.

If reality exists, it doesn't do so *a priori,* but only to be put together. Thus one might say reality is an activity, of which literature is part, an important part, but one among many.

Live as much in the moment as possible, to redress a balance. In the fifties, and for fifty years, we were paralyzed by the past: by history, by psychoanalysis, by myth, by our cultural heritage, by a kind of cultural neurosis—in the sense that neurosis can be considered the preservation of a traumatic past as the source of behavior no longer appropriate to the present. Our old systems of thought and behavior further obscure an almost incomprehensible present—like Bergson's theory of comedy. We must divest ourselves of all mechanical response, get rid of our habits. Quote from Wallace Stevens: "A violent order is disorder."

We improvise our novels as we improvise our lives.

The didactic job of the modern novel is to teach people to invent themselves and their world—Robbe-Grillet.

In fiction as in life, form arises as an idiosyncrasy, like an original work of art that can never be repeated. In this sense we must all become like artists, but artists of a risky art whose only convention is freedom.

The world is real because it is imagined. Thus philosophy should be stories. But stories are for children, though Plato chose that form. This is so because our conventional systems for formulating and dealing with reality, fiction included, have themselves become unreal. Only children would believe them. They are only stories.

Here the exact words of a comment by one of my students: Destroying the systems destroys the chaos. She had, as she put it, "walked right out of" a mental institution into my class to be-

come a brilliant poet and my good angel—we'll call her Angel.
Others were walking in the opposite direction, and with these kids
I had an immediate empathy. It's not such a bad idea to have a
nervous breakdown. There are many people in whom I would
provoke one if I could. Neal, for example, who was nominally a
graduate student, but who was slowly committing *de facto* suicide
by means of faster and faster sports cars, worse and worse acci-
dents. Neal would never have a nervous breakdown, he was too
rigid. He'd die first. Now in fact he's dead, he finally jumped off
a bridge. I used to sit around drinking coffee with him a lot. He
was very big on the Movement. He'd been beaten up in two
different demonstrations and by a Southern deputy-sheriff. But
it was a rather joyless commitment. He'd work himself up into
a rage talking about civil rights or Viet Nam, but fundamentally
they didn't mean a thing to him, and he knew it. And he'd say
it. Listen, he'd tell me, give me something that makes life worth
living. I'd usually start talking about girls, and that would get
into books, and we'd end up talking about politics, which would
send him into a rage finally, so that he'd take off in his car and
drive for a couple of hours, and I honestly never knew whether
I was going to see him alive again. He always wanted me to go
driving with him, but I absolutely refused. You're gonna kill
yourself one of these days man, do you know that? I know that,
he'd say. Why do you do it? I'd ask. He'd shrug: It makes life
interesting.

Today the man who takes care of the house did me a good
turn, which was not only nice, but was a demonstration of actual
concern. What did I expect of the old roast beef after all? What
did he know about snow dolmens? We are all spoiled children of
the same gross father, whether we like it or not.

At the bird bell we've had cardinals—the red male and orange
female, jays, tree sparrows, tufted titmice, white-breasted nuthatches, and slate-colored juncos. This morning a female downy
woodpecker dropped by for a peck or two, didn't like the taste,
and beat it. Come to think of it, I haven't seen the nuthatches for
a while—maybe they've gone further south because of the under-
zero weather. The cardinals too for that matter. Maybe we're being deserted. The crows are still around though. You see them flying across the snowy fields, like in a Breughel, or perched on a
solitary tree limb, thinking. I wish I had been educated by crows.

Crows are smart. They know how to think so that their thinking is part of their world, like a wing beat, like the wind. They sit there thinking what they know, and what they know is how to think without thought. Since I've started thinking about this story I've gotten boils, piles, eye strain, stomach spasms, anxiety attacks. Finally I am consumed by the thought that at a certain point we all become nothing more than dying animals. Some day one of these stories is going to be mortal, it's inevitable. Storyteller Strangled By Own Yarn. Why do all our inventions become Frankensteins? It's because we don't think right. We don't think like crows. Crows know how to think with their wings, and when they ponder it's a way of weighing their stillness. But I'll find a way, this marathon will become a way, until each thought becomes an act of creation, and life will seem what it is: a reward for some primal good deed.

Meanwhile my chief concern is whether I'm going to be able to sell this unprecedented example of formlessness. How can you sell a current in a river? Maybe I better put my editor into it, he's a terrific editor, maybe that'll do the trick. A few more plugs like that and he won't be able to afford not to publish it. Or how about a little sex, that's the ticket. That's what this needs. A little sex. Okay, a little sex.

My wife was out, my mistress was out of town, tied up for the last time I hoped with her husband—or could I now say ex-husband? I was waiting for my girlfriend, let's call her Teddy. She was fifteen. I had known her more briefly than I had known Betty, but I'd already put in a lot more time with her. It was already more gratifying, more frustrating, in short more intense, and above all, more interesting. Perhaps it was Teddy who was really my mistress. But then it seemed absurd to call a fifteen-year-old your mistress. Betty had a husband, or at least an ex-husband, and she was twenty-one—so I decided more or less arbitrarily to call Betty my mistress, and Teddy my girlfriend. Just to keep things straight. So. My wife was out, my mistress was away, I was waiting for my girlfriend. A little sex.

But first I have to go and get myself a supply of toothpicks. Why toothpicks? Because at that stage, though I had stopped smoking quite a while back, I had for various nervous reasons I won't go into here, though they might become evident, a great urge to start smoking cigarettes again. Which I did. I'm not a fanatic. Only, after my first sore throat I'd decided to substitute toothpicks. So at that time I was almost always chewing on some wet, bent, vulgar toothpick. Now Teddy, noticing this habit, and taking it no doubt as an integral part of my personality as well as, maybe, a fundamental element in my approach to life, at a certain point picked up a toothpick, examined one end, then the other, and stuck it in her mouth. After that, Teddy would meet me with a toothpick in her mouth and we would sit around offering toothpicks to one another in a comradely way, or even sharing them, the way lovers sometimes like to share the same cigarette. Now pay attention. Teddy, the fifteen-year-old, who comes to visit me with erotic intentions, the presumable virgin, or tabula rasa, as it were, observes my most casual habit, and like a disciple, or a monkey, slavishly mimics it. Add to this that there was always a certain amount of inevitable confusion on her part as to whether I was her lover or her father, and a certain amount of acknowledged confusion on mine as to whether or not she was my daughter. At last, the ultimate teaching situation. She always called me Professor Sukenick, even in our most intimate moments, not only because that was what she had begun by calling me, but as a real sign of respect and submissiveness. And I, for my part, did not want to disillusion her.

She knocks at the door. I open it and look at my watch. You're five minutes late, I said. Do you want another spanking? She smiles at me uncertainly. I relieve her of her briefcase, her pencil box, her coat, and wait while she removes her sweater and mini-skirt and hands them to me, which leaves her nude except for her sandals which I allow her to keep on. She is not allowed any underwear when she comes to visit, and must wear a mini-skirt—those are some of the rules. I then confiscate her clothing to a place known only to myself. There it remains till I want to give all or some of it back. One day I offer her a choice of two, and only two, articles of clothing, and so she went out in mini-skirt and pea-jacket. She's still standing nude in front of the door, waiting for my acknowledgment that the entry ritual has been completed.

May I come in now Professor Sukenick? she asks timidly.

Of course, Teddy. I was not unkindly to the girl. Have a toothpick. I often wondered what her parents thought of this new and disgusting habit of chewing toothpicks.

Can I make you a cup of tea or something, Professor? I was damn well sure she wasn't as polite to her father as I'd taught her to be to me.

No, just stand there while I feel you up for a while, I said, sitting down on the couch.

Do I have to?

Yes, I told her. And she did.

After five or ten minutes of this, though she wasn't given to making demands, she asked, breathing heavily, Would you like me to lie down now, Professor Sukenick?

Yes, I said. Go and lie on my desk. I went and got my polaroid camera.

We're going to have a little fun with nude modeling today, I told her. After that we can play doggie again if you like. Did you bring your leash?

How's that? Not bad? A little sex? Okay. Now let's do a retake of that, with a little more accuracy this time. But first a little background material. Narrative mode.

One evening, not so very long ago, I was standing around in the dimly lit lobby of an art theater, idly waiting for the show to change. A casual glance around the premises revealed the presence of numerous good-looking chicks, as usual, but mainly escorted. A few hot, furtive, follow-up glances singled out two or three really nice looking pieces, one of whom, I could not help but notice, kept throwing a bold eye in my direction from around her huge, round, dark glasses. What ho! thought I. She was a nice-looking bit of baggage, attired in the latest hip-chic style. Now what are you gonna do if every female in the city from twelve to fifty dresses in the same damn style? Meanwhile the glances, the smiles, the smirks, the takes, the winces, the ogles, the sneezes, the grimaces, the eye-flutterings, the nose-pullings, the hiccups, the winks, the nods, the head-shakes, the curl-tossing, the handkerchief-dropping, the posturing, the posing, the deep-breathing exercises, the giggling, the hemming, the hawing, the burping, the nose-quivering, the eye-rolling, the lip-writhing, the cheek-puffing, the lid-lifting, the head-hanging, the arm-lashing, the gesturing, the gesticulating, the gymnastics, the calisthenics, continued to be directed my way. In any case, I had the impression that she was trying to make me aware of her presence. I began drifting toward her as she had seemed toward me. And before you know it, on some cheap pretense, I had her locked in awkward conversation about trivia, the upshot of which was, that she'd be happy to have my company during the movie. Immediately whereupon, we entered the darkened auditorium, and took two seats in the farthest corner well to the rear. Well, it was, not strangely, like making out with a girl on a high school movie date. I kept speculating as to how far she would "let me go." Without going into the gory details, I will say that I had a cock-rousing time of it. I kept thinking, man I hope this chick has an apartment without roommates, preferably close by. Well, the movie ended and we got outside under a streetlight and I did a double take. Then I thought, no no, she's just a young looking twenty-one. We didn't talk much up to then, but what she'd said seemed smarter than what most twenty-one-year-olds had to say. Well we walked down the block a while. I took another look. Well, maybe she was eighteen. Finally I said, Hey just as a matter of curiosity, how old are you actually?

She looked at me and gulped. What would you say? she asked.

Thirty, I said.

She laughed. No, really.

Fifteen.

She nodded. How did you know? she said. People never guess my age like that.

Hey wait a minute, I said. I was only kidding.

How old are you? she asked.

Thirty-four.

I looked at her. Now I could see it. Fifteen. It fitted her exactly. She did look fifteen, after all, if you looked at her with fifteen in mind.

I thought you might be over thirty, she said.

Well, that was that. I took her for a polite cup of coffee, with impenetrable awkward silences, between which I discovered that she lived up on Central Park East, attended a well-known private school, and that she wanted to be an artist, a sculptor, to be exact. And that she had promised her father to be home by twelve midnight. Since it was eleven forty-five, we went outside and I hailed her a cab, for which her father had given her money. I suspect there's a bear around here. Big, heavy tracks around the house, then back up the mountain into the woods, don't know what else could be that big. I've seen them around before.

They say there are strays around here, sometimes. After all we're surrounded by a huge state forest.

This story works on the principle of simultaneous multiplicity, or the knack of keeping several things on your mind at once. That is the central fact of our mental atmosphere. That is the water in which we swim, or should I say, the stew in which we cook. What we have to become is master jugglers, perfect a balancing act. We have to become artists in the sense that circus performers are called artists, equilibrists who can do seven things at once without thinking about it. Because we've already thought about it. Or because our sages have already thought about it, thought it all out, and we've learned it from them. Make it look easy, show us the easy way, easier and easier. Let peasants enslave themselves to the difficult.

We're at a seance. You the participants, I the medium in face of the total blank nothingness of uncreation.

I can't go on.

Go on.

Nothing. Muscle spasms. Bowel pains. Galloping migraine symptoms. I've got to stop.

Go on.

I have the impulse to get up and do a wild dance of pain. I squirm, sweat. Hands on either side of me hold me in my seat. I can't. I can't. Nothing. Nothing.

Suddenly a voice says: Everyone can fly. The voice my own.

Ah come on, they say. What do you call that, what does that mean?

Jesus Christ, I say, isn't that enough? Come on, let me go.

Keep going. Keep going. Go on.

Suddenly the letter J. Why J? J is a bird. A bird that mimics other birds. Perhaps because its own voice is so imperious, so demanding, that it would rather deny it. J. J, J, the voice says. It appears to be about three inches above and behind my left ear.

J. J. walks down the street. He's tall, a little husky and seems, perhaps without reason, to strut a bit, moving with a curious gawking swing to his head and neck. Seems to be about thirty, balding, but with a tuft of hair sticking up on the back of his head. The street is odd too, because it's just a street, that is, there are no buildings along it, no traffic, no people, no scenery, a

street disappearing in a grey haze in the middle distance with
nothing on either side, nothing in front, nothing behind. Now
there are buildings, brownstones. J. J. lives in a brownstone: two
rooms on the fourth floor. He has just brought his garbage down.
An occasional car passes along the street, always in the same
direction, the street is evidently one way. An elderly woman
comes down the opposite sidewalk carrying a shopping bag. She
clutches her coat to the breast. J. J. too wears an overcoat, but
no gloves, no muffler, no hat it must be the fall, or just possibly
early spring, one would say the fall because of the tree growing
out of the sidewalk with a little fence around it which has nothing
but a few brown leaves hanging from its boughs. J. J. stops to
light a cigarette.

I can't go on.

Go on.

To light a cigarette. He reaches into his pocket for his pack,
takes one, and puts it into his mouth. But just as he is searching
for a book of matches, a portly man in a grey felt hat, rather
distingué, comes over and holds up a cigarette lighter, one of
those gas jet jobs.

Hi there, he booms.

J. J. lights his cigarette from the lighter.

How are you, says the portly man.

Uh, fine, says J. J. And you?

The weather's getting on, says the portly man. Well, take care.
He walks on down the street.

Who was that? J. J. wonders. Possibly the landlord? He can
never remember the landlord's face. Even now he's forgotten
what the portly man looked like. Was he portly? It must have
been the landlord. Was the landlord portly? The street is lined
with parked cars. J. J. walks ahead for a while, then stops next
to one of the cars, gets in, and then slides over behind the wheel.
He begins feeling through his pockets for keys.

I can't go on.

Go on.

Suddenly a fiery redheaded red-faced man runs up, and rips
open the door.

What are you doing in my car? Get out of there.

Oh, awfully sorry, says J. J. He gets out feeling awkward. The
man looks at him suspiciously.

You see, begins J. J., I have a sixty-three Ford, a red one, just exactly like this one.

This is a Chevrolet, says the man.

They looked so much alike that year, says J. J.

This is a sixty-six, says the man. And in any case it's green, as you can see.

Well you know I wasn't trying to steal your car, said J. J., there's no need to worry. I can't drive in any case.

Oh, well, says the man. I didn't really suspect anything. Of course these things happen.

Yes, said J. J.

The redheaded man took out a pack of cigarettes. Cigarette? he asked J. J.

Oh no thank you, J. J. said. Thank you, no. I never smoke. All right enough of this. I'm not filibustering fate, like Beckett or one of those cats. This is not a game it's a story. Or it's both, a game and a story. Or . . . But then who cares what it is?

The kids were sitting around the cafeteria, playing Mah-Jongg and listening to rock 'n' roll. That was their latest camp thing. If they weren't reading comic books they were always playing some kind of game: bridge, Monopoly, Scrabble, steal the old man's pack, chinese checkers, dominos, and always with the rock 'n' roll. Some kid was always coming up with some new horrible old game. Checkers, canasta, ugh. It all came out of a kind of considered boredom.

How can they sit around like that? asked Neal. It's disgusting. I couldn't sit around like that. Bunch of freaks. He was practically bouncing up and down on his seat in exasperation. Johnson's already dropping bombs on Hanoi and they sit around like a bunch of happy morons.

They're not happy and they're not morons, I said. Besides, what are you gonna do about Hanoi?

I don't know, I don't even really give a shit. Just give me something else to do with my life, that's all.

Why don't you just try to relax and be happy? I told him.

What do I care about being happy, he snapped.

America is probably the one place in the world where you get the idea of justice mixed up with the idea of happiness. Actually they corrupt one another. Why didn't you come to my classes on Henry Miller?

I read Henry Miller. He says everything has got to blow up. That's the way I feel about it.

Take Dog-tongue Mike for example. Look at him. He's happy as hell. You couldn't find a happier guy. And he's as engagé as you are.

He's a moron.

All right. But he's the right kind of moron.

Mike had just walked into the cafeteria. I waved to him. As a teacher you wind up liking all sorts of kids who hate one another's guts. Mike came over and sat down. He was a mouth-breather. His lips were wet and his tongue, which was quite pink, and pointed, was always lolling out of one corner of his mouth. He panted as he listened to you, and every now and then you could actually see a drop of saliva fall off the tip of his tongue, after which he would lick his lips profusely with a slurping sound. His dark-brown eyes were always rolling around in his head, showing a lot of white eyeball, and he had a bush of thick curly hair like an unclipped black poodle. He had a thick, muscular figure, and he was an amazing lecher. His thing was two or even three girls at a time. He was always walking around with a little harem, different ones, I don't know where he found them all. At about that point Betty sailed in like Miss America, only in tight jeans and some guy's black leather jacket. She floated over to our table through the upper layers of the ionosphere.

So whatayagot eyes? Mike asked me.

Ah come on, said Neal.

Whatayamean? asked Mike. She's not a bad piece (slurp).

I am happy to report that the cardinals and the nuthatches are still around. I'm especially happy about the cardinals as the orange female and the red male look so good against the snow. The brilliance of the cardinal was one of nature's bold strokes, one of her masterpieces. There's one of the ideas we have to get rid of: the Great Work. That's one of the ways we have of strangling ourselves in our culture. We've got enough Great Works. Once a work becomes Great forget it. What we need is not Great Works but playful ones in whose sense of creative joy everyone can join. Play, after all, is the source of the learning instinct, that has been proved by indisputable scientific experiments. And what characterizes play? Freedom, spontaneity, pleasure. This is as distinguished from games, games are formu-

larized play. I've always had a prejudice against games, I got
stuck at some infantile pre-game stage. I like to make up my own
games. And anyway, what games are there today that you can
play without a sense of camp, which is to say, without a sense of
hollowness, meaninglessness, self-consciousness—a ploy against
the abyss? And self-conscious pleasure is perverted pleasure, ultimately nihilistic. No, we have to invent new games—and then
discard them and invent more. This, then, is the beginning of our
literary re-education. A story is a game someone has played so
that you can play it too, and having learned how to play it,
throw it away. All good books are both didactic and gratuitous.
I want to write a book that will teach things I don't know.

John Johnson was a short, slight fellow, tall and portly, with
a nondescript face, except for the scar that seamed his left
temple, cut across his left eye, grazed the left corner of his mouth,
and cleft his chin in two unequal parts. This, as John would tell
you in the most casual encounter, was a dueling scar, although it
really wasn't. It was so prominent that people remembered the
scar, and not John's face. So nobody ever remembered what John
really looked like. Similarly, John was always going on fanatic
diets or, alternately, frantically trying to gain weight, so that at
times he appeared bloated and overbearing, and at other times
self-effacing to the point of virtual nonexistence. This proved
confusing to his friends, who had great trouble recognizing John
from one time to another, but actually it wasn't so bad, because
John didn't have any friends. That was John all over.

You could find John all over town. In fact you might say he
was a man about town. John had the money to be a man about
town. And he had the time. And he had the talent to be a man
about town. John had it all over everybody when it came to being
a man about town.

But unfortunately it was all over for poor John. And I'll tell
you why.

John had no watchacall stick-to-itiveness. He'd walk out of
his house in the morning, or at night, or some other time, with a
sure stride, and a look of determination on his face. He'd hail a
cab, or maybe get on a bus, or on a subway, whichever happened
to come along first, or maybe he'd get into a car, which, since
he didn't have a car, was usually somebody else's. But the thing
was that, no sooner was John on his way than he'd forget where

he was going. So that, for example, if he were on the subway, he might end up at Woodside Avenue in the Bronx, get out, and wander around till he was hungry enough to look for an Automat or something. Oh, he had good intentions, John did. But they all seemed somehow to go wrong. For example, he'd get into a cab, slam the door, the cabbie would ask, Where to buddy? John would sit there for a minute, then he'd say, I changed my mind, I think I'll walk. In that way John frequently got his ass beat off, and some people even say that was how he got his scar. Another thing is that once out of his house, John could never remember where he lived, so that he was often picked up off the streets by policemen late at night, stumbling around half frozen, unless it were the summer. Also John Johnson never could quite remember who he was, so that if by chance he met one of his friends, who would come up to him and say, Hello there, John Johnson, he would look over his shoulder and say, Who? Or if another one of his friends by chance came up to him and said, Say, aren't you John Johnson? he would look at him and say, I don't know. Am I? But that was all right really since John Johnson didn't have any friends, and maybe that was the reason.

agreement may give the 1968 victory to the Republicans the other meeting is backing Senator Eugene McCarthy of Minnesota who is challenging President Johnson on Vietnamese policy one of the biggest stories of the Vietnamese war is going on without anyone being anything said about it officially they say American planes have been hammering hard at the Ho Chi Minh trail which connects North and South Viet Nam via Laos Laos is officially neutral in the Vietnamese war and that's why the United States official silence the informants say the United States Air Force is sending about two hundred fifty fighter bombers a day to blast increasing

fleets of trucks and other vehicles
channeling supplies down the trail
through Laos Viet Nam Lt. General Robert Cushman has come
out strongly against any halt
American bombings of North
Viet Nam even for five minutes as
he put it in an interview at Danang
today he pictured the Vietnamese
war as involving what he calls a
main force which is supplied by
Red China and the Soviet Union

"The law requires you to fill out and return this questionnaire
on or before the date shown to the right above in order that your
local board will have current information to enable it to classify
you."

"Other occupational qualifications including hobbies I possess
are" pyromania, vandalism, homicide.

I've never been able to figure out whether these questions are
supposed to get you in the Army or keep you out of it. "I speak
fluently the following foreign languages or dialects": Urdu,
Finno-Ugric, and pig latin. "I read and write well the following
foreign languages or dialects": hieroglyphics, bird calls, and
codes when I catch one.

"If you have any physical or mental condition which in your
opinion will disqualify you for service in the armed forces state
the condition." Enraged slip enlarged spleen, caused by total
political exacerbation. Whether this is a mental or physical condition is debatable.

The long dirty finger poked its way into my mailbox today.
What is this, routine? harassment? or the first signs of retaliation
for complicity in the resistance movement? People like me always
exist in some fundamental sense underground, but a few years
ago the time seemed ripe to come out in the open and choose
sides. I don't think it's been a tactical error, but if so it's been a
healthy one, and that has to be considered too. The risks, repression prison exile, are no longer so farfetched since they are
already closing in around people I know. But the stakes are now
too high to sit out the game. Dear folks, well it is not as bad as
you'd think, and I get a chance to put in a lot of sleep. I have a

very amusing cellmate, Sal the Schlung Palermo. Sal the Schlung, as we call him, is an interesting fellow, though not too heavy on conversation. He spends most of his time farting, and the rest of it whacking off like a maniac. I count it exceptionally fortunate to find myself in the intimacy of a type of person whom I might otherwise never have become acquainted with. The cell is permeated with the mingled odors of feculence and moldy sperm. I chalk it up to experience.

I am now going to give you a census of the Lower East Side in its heyday, or at least in my heyday. Avenue B. Upper Avenue B of course. Regis, our super, two wives, one dead, one somewhere else, several children, also somewhere else, no teeth, canny, quick, smooth, slow, cool, fast hand for a put-on, goatish, knows how to talk, busy cooking up a pot of something for supper, what he calls on the spur of the moment, "beef get-together." Drinks too much. Mr. Duke. About the same shade of color as Regis, about the same age as Regis, fifty, seventy, whatever it is, lives alone like Regis, dignified, splenetic, high blood pressure, lies dead, bloated and purple upstairs on the floor of his apartment, been there for a week. People thought he was out of town if they thought about him at all. Drank too much. Blazer. Small, dark, very hip, energetic Negro, out on bail for heroin possession, claims frame-up. Arresting officer kept hitting him in the stomach while making minute references to the sexual organs of the defendant's wife, cross-examining said defendant as to his attitude toward them, said wife happening to be a nice Irish girl. Several old Polish ladies with heart conditions living alone. Various leathery old ethnic ladies of an eternal nature. A Puerto Rican lady who had an illegitimate daughter who also had an illegitimate daughter. A Latino family of exemplary stability, soon to break up. A nice young pretty ex-middle-class well-mannered sexy blond junky, suitable for frame-up, who was a stool pigeon for the narcos. A tall silent old Oriental personage who looked very hard at all the girls. Every now and then a well-dressed young man would show up and take him off in a big hurry in a taxi or an anonymous-looking four-door sedan. A poorly dressed middle-aged man with five daughters who was always standing outside, didn't work, never said anything and looked right through you when you said hello. His wife, who was always screaming at him and at their daughters, especially when he or she got drunk.

They were the respectable family in the house. A strange man who always had two days' beard and always wore a suit, sometimes without a shirt, filthy, a mutterer, who slept on newspapers in the doorway to the roof. Lewis, a very pretty, peroxide-blond faggot interior decorator, who lived in the house next door and once burned it down in a pet, dispossessing all the tenants, and bringing to light strange pale specimens who crumbled to a disgusting white dust at the first breath of fresh air. The Jukes and the Kallikaks, his cousins, all of whom bore a certain family resemblance whether or not they were related, local ne'er-do-wells, born and bred on the Avenue, a jolly crew, always with one or more broken limbs in consequence of drunken fights, they sometimes out of their comradery favored the neighborhood with music from their own slap-dash band consisting of a two string guitar, a broken drum, a bent trumpet, a kazoo, a comb in tissue paper, a bongo, and an optional number of garbage-can tops, none of which any of them could play. Their good fellowship when juiced sometimes extended to one or more of a similar group of Puerto Rican *borrachones,* unshaven limping one-eyed lowlifes like out of a Bunuel movie, with that peculiar Hispanic combination of unspeakable viciousness and unbelievable cowardice which constitutes the last degraded depth to which *machismo* can sink. Harmless all in all, but they talked a lot, and threatened a lot of fights which they never got into. Moose, the unbelievably rapacious second-hand man who was my great enemy for stinking up the neighborhood and especially my apartment with his paint remover. Jorge the poet, who walked around with an old Rommel cap and a peggy leg, pushing a cart, and who was the greatest Puerto Rican poet resident in New York, and who recited poems, and who had a coconut that talked and sang, and who claimed he worked in the post office for seventeen years, and who was also an artist, and who painted signs. A dark woman dressed in black with livid face who walked swiftly through the streets and who had glittering teeth and red red lips, who would shake her fist at you and scream in a terrible maniac voice, God love you, God love you. The tailor who I avoid because of an argument about something he cleaned badly. The man in the paint store who I avoid because he found out I bought my paint somewhere else. The shoemaker who is a character out of Sholem Aleichem and has a photographic memory, and who I avoid

because there are too many complications over getting a pair of
heels replaced so I go to the Italian around the corner. The
grocery-store man who I avoid because of an argument over not
shopping at his store enough and going to the supermarkets all
the time. The druggist who I avoid because he's off his rocker and
comes on with advice like he's a doctor and probably performs
illegal operations in the back, or would like to. The fat bookie
who I avoid because I'm afraid of gangsters. The thin bookie
who I avoid for the same reason. Allen Ginsberg who I often see
walking up and down the Avenue eyes always averted I wonder
why, looking shrewd as a saint. One day he left his cigarettes on
the corner newsstand why didn't I pick them up and run after him
saying, Mr. Ginsberg, Mr. Ginsberg, Allen, here, you left your
cigarettes on the newsstand. We could have become great friends.
I too could have become as shrewd as a saint. Maybe I will. The
countermen in the corner candy store, magnificent in their rude-
ness. The Polish bartender across the street who founded a
bartending empire on the beatniks moving into the neighborhood,
and then the hippies, and then the diggers and then the yippies.
And the ersatz expresso-joint Bohemians on Tenth Street, schle-
miehl hippies, manqué social workers, who tried to make it on
the same crowd. The calm intelligence of the waiters in the cheap
Polish restaurant on Avenue A. The little Greek who ran a
restaurant and had statues of the gods above his cash register. The
sad-looking girl with the big boobs and the beautiful face and the
nice little kid who for some reason I never got to know, maybe I
will. The girl who walked down Avenue B one day wearing
nothing but a man's white T-shirt that came down barely below
her buttocks and no undies. The blond girl with no arms and no
legs who not only gets around but manages to be sexy as hell. The
gigantic seven-foot junkie who every year seems to turn up minus
another limb. The strange fellow with the weird shoes who stands
on street corners for hours in the coldest weather wearing nothing
but the same black cotton suit-jacket and who walks when he
walks down the middle of the Avenue with a weird gait like a
marionette, and takes the cake as far as I can see as the loneliest
person in the world. And on and on through the rest of the
doomsday book, which might not be a bad title for this chronicle.

New subject. Or as the chef replied when asked about the
seasoning, Thyme for a change. Keep moving. Where? Nowhere,

as fast as possible. Which is just about the state of things chronic
and cosmic. This is just a long solo man, a solo flight, part of our
immense solar drift that eddies through the hurtling universe. Go
baby. Catch up with yourself.

She had to be home by twelve midnight. We went outside and
I hailed a cab for her. I held the door open.

Will we ever see one another again? she asked.

No, I said. Come on, I'll ride uptown with you.

We had a chatty driver. He had a theory about traffic flow in
Manhattan.

Boy lemme tellya something, he began. I'm on nights, five
nights a week, right? Six if I work overtime. Right? Right?

Yeah, yeah, right.

Lemme tellya something, if you subtracted all the people I
pick up in that time where I picked you up down in the Village
and drop where I'm dropping you up on the Upper East Side, you
be subtracting a lot of people.

That right.

Oh boy, lemme tellya, you be subtracting a lot of people. A lot
of people. Right? You know what I mean? Right?

Yeah, yeah, right.

I don't know what it is but it's like a kind of Appalachian Trail,
you know what I mean? People come down from the Central
Park East area to the Village, and then they come up from the
Village to the Central Park East area like it was a regular
Appalachian Trail. If you subtracted those fares, you be sub-
tracting one hell of a lot of fares, you know what I mean? Right?

Yeah, right, right. I turned to Teddy.

So whaddya goin up town? Huh?

Yeah, I said. Listen, what did you have in mind, did you think
we were going to start dating or something? I mean don't you
think I'm a little too old for you? I had my arm around her,
automatically resuming the physical intimacy that had begun in
the movie.

I don't see what age has to do with it, she said without batting
an eyelash.

Well you know for one thing, I'm used to making love with
girls I'm going with, I told her. She twitched slightly.

That's all right, she said.

What?

I mean, that comes as a matter of course. She didn't talk like I thought a fifteen-year-old talked.

Doesn't it? she asked.

Well, yes, I said. I started kissing her lips, then stopped. This is absurd, I said. She smiled at me. I kissed her again.

So whaddya live up there? said the cab driver. We were caught in a traffic jam.

You can take it easy, I told him. I'm not in a hurry.

He's not in a hurry, he said.

Besides, I said, I have a wife you know. I felt her twitch again.

I guessed you did, she said.

Doesn't that make any difference to you? I asked.

No. Why should that make any difference? I'm not going to marry you.

Are you thought of as exceptional? I asked.

I don't know, she said. Do you love her?

Who my wife? Yes. She licked her lips. What are you thinking? I asked.

Are we going to see one another again?

I don't know. Give me your number. I'll see. Frankly I doubt it. I'm very busy. She wrote her number out for me.

Is it because I'm young? she asked.

No. I'll do anything if it's interesting.

Don't you think I'm interesting?

Yes, I do. And you're pretty too.

Then it's because of the sex thing?

Well there are laws you know.

Why do people always have their minds on sex? she asked. It just comes in the course of things, isn't that true?

Not necessarily for people your age, I said. Besides, your parents might not approve.

They'll never know. Because I won't tell them. Besides they know I have a lot of older friends. They let me do what I want to anyway. They even let me go out alone at night like this, as long as I'm going to some place specific.

To make love with someone for instance.

I think my father might actually understand, she said thoughtfully. But I wouldn't tell him. It's none of his business. I have my own life. Her father was a big architect whose name I'd recognized. He'd been in the news a lot around then for designing what he called a Vertical Suburb, a self-contained skyscraper living unit that could be installed safely in the midst of the most blighted city.

I'll take advantage of you, I said.

How?

I didn't answer, because I didn't know.

We were pulling up to a huge apartment building facing the Park.

So whaddya dropping the girl?

Will you call me? she asked.

If you give me a really nice kiss, I said, I might.

A doorman opened the taxi door. We grabbed one another and she gave me a really nice kiss, a long, surprising kiss.

Promise? she asked.

I promised.

I've had three different long-distance phone conversations today whose main topic was prosecution of people involved in resistance to the war. People are actually at the stage of leaving for the Canadian border overnight. I'd probably pick jail if it came to it, but I can't really believe it will come to it. But then I couldn't really believe it would come to this a few months ago. The draft calls are going up every month. They're scraping forty thousand. They're trying to draft a guy I know who's thirty-seven because of his part in the resistance. My sense of time is askew. It seems to me there's been a gradual acceleration that began some years ago, and whose increasing momentum only became discernible in the relatively recent past. It seems to me that I can already almost hear the sound of time as it whines howls shrieks into a future that is becoming explosively compressed, like the shock wave in front of a jet approaching the sound barrier, and we are left desperately trying to catch up, catch up with time, with history, with our lives, with our experience, with our very selves, before

Betty came and stood next to our table. Hi, she said blandly. Mike grabbed her tight pants at the left buttock. Have a seat, he said (slurp).

Cut it out, she said with a kind of *pro forma* indignation. Squirming away, she laughed mildly.

Watch yourself, Neal told him, or I'll call the A.S.P.C.A. They'll put you out of your misery.

Not me, said Mike. I'm happy.

You've fucked your brains out through your cock, that's your thing, said Neal.

Well like they say, said Mike, as long as you're happy, right? I mean I believe in putting our sex right on the table.

We all gazed at his fly expectantly.

Not right now, please, said Betty with a mock-genteel shudder.

I mean you should watch my dogs, he said. Mike bred and sold some enormous kind of thoroughbred dog as a way of supporting himself in college. Irish Wolfhounds I think. When they meet first thing they get acquainted with one another's asses and genitals. Now that makes some sense I think. I mean here we are sitting around this table arguing ideas and the real truth is everybody wants to fuck everybody, right? (Slurp, slurp.)

Perhaps I'd better leave, said Betty looking around. I mean I'm not quite ready to stand still for a gang bang. She smiled at me.

Sex is all right, said Neal, till you stop coming. Then what?

I'm not talking about that, said Mike. I'm talking about a whole new non-middle-class attitude toward your body. The body is no longer private property.

No longer property, corrected Betty. It's still private. At least this one is, she said hugging herself with her arms.

Not private, I said. Personal. Totally personal. We've got to stop being depersonalized.

That's not cool, said Neal.

Yes it is, I say. That's what you want to stay cool for. To keep a grip on your self literally. To hold on to yourself as against the threat of the impersonal. See what I mean?

I see it, said Neal. I don't know if I believe it. It just makes you more vulnerable.

I like that, said Betty. My body isn't private, it's personal.

I'll keep that in mind, I said.

There's an idea that could have results, said Mike. (Slurp.)

You eat yet? I asked her.

I'm not eating today.

Why don't we go for a walk, I said.

She's not walking today, she's flying, said Neal.

Now the fact that he had no friends was a source in Jim Jones of considerable depression and pain. This is the story of how Jim Jones went about trying to find himself some friends.

A thorough person, Jim decided that he had better begin at the beginning by finding out exactly what friends were. With this in mind, he went to the dictionary, and located the word "friend," which was between "fried cake" and "friend at court," where he discovered that a "friend" was a more complicated thing than he had imagined. A "friend" was "one attached to another by feelings of personal regard." But it was also a well-wisher, a patron or supporter, and it was also "one who was on good terms with another, one not hostile," and it was also "a member of the same nation, party," and it was also "a member of the Society of Friends, the Christian sect opposed to taking oaths and to war, founded by George Fox about 1650." His mind reeling with the foregoing complexities, Jim Jones tucked his dictionary under his arm and went out into the street. In a short time Jim encountered a man and a woman walking amorously arm in arm. This seemed to him to fit the first definition of a "friend," "one attached to another by feelings of personal regard." However, here Jim came on an unexpected problem: Which one of them was the "friend"? He opened his dictionary and checked. "One attached to another" was all the dictionary said. At the last moment Jim lunged in front of the couple, stopping them in their course down the street. Friend, he shouted at the startled pair, which, which, which one of you is a friend? Don't panic Etta, the man said to the woman. Stay behind me. The two backed off slowly down the street, and after a certain distance turned around and ran.

Jim Jones opened the dictionary again, and read down through the definition, all the way down to "friendless, adj.," and "friend-lessness, n.," including "syn.: companion, comrade, chum, crony; see acquaintance." Which one? Jim asked himself, for Jim no more had any acquaintances than he had friends. Is it any wonder that Jim Jones is a lonely, embittered man, living in isolation from his neighbors, his compatriots, his associates, his companions, his acquaintances, his comrades, his chums, his cronies, his friends, his ancestors, his forebears, his three giraffes, his two monkeys, and his platypus? Each evening at six P.M., when other folks were busy burrowing into the bosoms of their wives, or

bosoming into the burrows of their families, in boroughs all
over the city, namely, Brooklyn, the Bronx, Queens, Manhattan,
and Richmond, Jim Jones invariably found himself, like the
others, hurrying home from his job, until he remembered that he
had no job. This left him what you might call up in the air. Still,
out of inertia as much as anything else, Jim continued hurrying
home—but then, where did he live? Jim hadn't the faintest idea.
Cleverly, he thought of looking himself up in the phone book,
but then, under what name would he look himself up? It seemed
to him that his name began with a K. Or an A. "Axel Kassel,"
perhaps. Or "Anders Kidney." Or "Kid Actual." Oh Jim Jones!
Six hundred and fifty thousand words in the English language,
and none of them to call you by? Except possibly "Jock Josephs"?
or "Jimmy Jerusalem"? Or "Janek Johanssen"?

Poor Jim Jones didn't know what to do with himself. He didn't
even know what his self was. Was it, evasively, "a person or thing
referred to with respect to individuality, one's own person"? Or,
even worse, "one's nature, character, etc."? "Personal interest,
selfishness"? Or was it, most philosophically, "the individual consciousness in relation to itself"? These didn't help. Ah Jim Jones,
you lack common sense. Be yourself, that's my advice, just be
yourself. But how could he, when he didn't know what it was?
Talk into the microphone.
What was that clever thing I
said that gave me the impulse
to tape this?
Deep? No.
No. I don't know if you're
being picked up. Say something.
What was the clever thing?
Oh I signed the complicity
oath and I also signed the
oath in complicity with the
people who are in complicity
therefore I'm in complicity
with myself.
Graham?
Oh Phil's.
Yeah, isn't it.

Yeah, hold it, oh I know why
you're not coming through,
because, because I've got the
thing on the mouthpiece, and I
think I must have expected, I
must have expected your voice
to come to come out through my
mouth through my ear through
my mouth.
Wait a minute now I'm gonna
do it through, how can I hear
you, wait a minute now I've
got the microphone, can you
hear me?
Ah now you're coming through,
say something.

Yeah.
That's nice.

give me that you just want to
record yourself.

You have your choice.

Hear me now or hear me later.
I met Mr. Beaver of Beaver
Books.
He's a very decent man.
Uh, very decent, very nice, I
liked him. And uh I met him
inadvertently in fact I didn't
understand who he was at first
it took me a while and uh once
I realized who he was I plugged
Green's book to him and I think
it may have worked.

You mean for paperback? Phil's
book has just gone into paper
back, he just sold the paper
back rights. To Schocken books
which is very little but you
know

They're good yeah. It's not
gonna be a best seller in any
case so what's the difference?

Hm. What does he do?

Oh.

Yeah they're a good company
though

Right.
But anyway Beaver is really a
good guy.

He's working for his old man
now I think.

Hm. This is like tapping your
own wire.

Tapping your own wire, is that
the uh title of your new
novelette?

That's not a bad idea, that's
like being in conspiracy with
yourself, to tap your own wire.
I think I better break out of
this somehow I think I'm gonna
make the beep sound now:
Beep.

Okay listen look this phone
call is costing me a mint.
A mint.

No, I'll tell you something
about these phone calls to New
York, or from New York. On
the one hand they cost more
than you think they do, but on
the other hand they don't cost
as much as you think they will
after you think they after you
realize they're gonna cost more
than you think you would've,
they would've, to begin with,
if you follow me.

Well remember to call me back.

Yeah I'll call you back.
Actually you just beat me to it
because I was on the point of
calling you. But, but

U-u-m.

all right let's make it some
time next week.

Very good because I really
wanna see you.
Great.

Maybe Monday.
Okay, it may have to be without Lynn this time because she
has a kind of frantic schedule
and I'm not sure if it's gonna

With or without Lynn. Like
with or without whipped cream.

All right I'll call you when I'm
in New York.

Okay, Lynn says hello hello.

You what?
You want one a what collage?
You want one of Lynn's
Collages. Oh. Okay. I'll tell
her.
Okay.
No.
Okay. Goodbye.

And, yes, and Bosa says hello
hello.

And uh I wanna know if uh uh
I want one of Lynn's collages.
I want one of Lynn's collages.
I want one of Lynn's collages.
Collages.

Okay.
Okay, anything else?
Okay.
Right. Goodbye.

Well, how was that? In the literary sense I mean? Art imitates
life, n'est-ce pas? But why am I always baiting my readers? That's
a nasty habit. This is not *Notes from the Underground* after all.
Why am I so hostile and defensive? I'll never get to be as shrewd
as a saint that way. From now on I'm going to be completely
open with you my friend, as wide open as the form of this performance. You may cut me down in my tracks, you, reader, may
close the book or worse, not even buy it, you, editor, may not
even publish it, you, agent, may not even try to sell it. I stand
before you nude and defenseless, my naked soul quivering in the
below-zero cold. Exhibitionist. All right come on, cut the wise
cracks, give us the goods. Seriously, what I mean to say is, as the
tempo of this chronicle becomes more and more frantic, as it
begins to consume my life so that day by day, hour by hour, there
is more and more of my life in it than there is left out of it,
period end of sentence. Oh there are still quite a few little things
that I leave out, I'm not really an exhibitionist after all, or if so, a
crafty one, but fewer and fewer. For one thing, I do very little
else now besides work on this story, so there's very little else to
put in. Is this life becoming art? Or is it art becoming life? Does
it matter? The only thing that matters is to keep going from
moment to moment, as quick and fluid and surprising as one
moment flowing continuously into the next.

Here's a digression. But that's silly, when there's no plot line
there are no digressions. Life doesn't proceed by causal sequence,
except in hindsight, which gives a false view. Destroying the

systems destroys the chaos, right? What I'm getting at is, the first
time Teddy came to visit me, she came with a beautiful young
friend and contemporary, a slight, gorgeous blond named Jeanie.
Don't get excited, this is not a scene out of *Blow-up*. I want to kill
some funny ideas you're probably getting about me right now
while I think of it. I'm not a sex fiend, first of all, I don't have a
Lolita complex. Young girls in general have no appeal for me,
fat legs and dirty knees, blah. I do other things besides making
it with girls, lots of them. At this very time, I was writing two
books at once, and teaching is very hard work too although you
may not know it. I don't know where I found time for all this
stuff. Finally, I'm a strict monogamist who looks on divorce and
adultery with much the same kind of repulsion that some of the
younger pot, speed, and acid heads feel, a little puritanically, I
think, toward alcohol and tobacco. I've just redefined the terms,
that's all. With a wave of the hand. That's all it takes. I do what
interests me and I do what's fun and I juggle it all around and
try to balance it out. It's a balancing act. Sometimes it works,
sometimes it flops. You know a better way? Then again sex is a
terrific way of getting to know people. I mean really know people.
There's very little communion going on these days outside of
church, and none inside it. Sex carries a heavier load than it
ought to for me I know, for all of us. Has a lot to do with the
failure of other institutions, means of communication, corruption
of words. Sex is becoming overloaded and it's going to become a
bore soon if we don't look out. Like with these kids, to get back
to where I started. With Jeanie, for example, she went through
all that stuff so young that she wasn't even interested in sex much
any more really. It's true that a gang bang she was trapped into
when she was fourteen led to a certain scepticism on her part
about a lot of things, but that's not what I mean. Making love for
her was like, as she put it, if you go to the beach you go swimming, that's part of it. That's not what she was interested in, what
she was interested in was affection she could trust, being taken
care of in a way she could accept, and finding out about things
she didn't understand—in other words in a mother and father.
She had absolutely no idea of what was real, though she was very
sharp on what wasn't, for example, when she found out I'm a
novelist she said, I don't read many novels, they never tell the
truth. But her mother and father were just as up tight as she was.

In fact they were in a panic. At this stage, they literally locked
her up at night, and a little later, because of some infraction, they
locked her up in the daytime too, except for school. So naturally,
since they locked her up, she decided to escape, and she ran
away from home, came down to the Village, was kept by a bunch
of acid heads for a while, was passed around for a while, and
when they finally found her she was really messed up. Teddy told
me that she was finally institutionalized—she thought all her
boyfriends were out to kill her. I would like to come back to
Jeanie sometime. Someday, I thought, some September morning
at 11 o'clock, as I glance at the class list from the registrar, she
will walk in, sit down in the last seat in the farthest corner, put
her pocketbook on the floor, and gaze out the window, thin, pale,
needing everything and expecting very little, waiting for someone
to say something she can believe.

Well I got into that kind of thing with Teddy. We used to go
down to the McDougal Street coffee shops a lot and I'd meet
these kids there. Nobody noticed the age difference down there,
and anyway she didn't look that young, especially in that milieu.
She had two ways of talking, conversation and prattling. Conversation quickly became easy and interesting. We fell on the
same side of some generational continental divide. She didn't
have to talk up and I didn't have to talk down, or *vice versa,* I
don't think. The prattling was when she would just rattle on and
on about her life and her friends and her school and her parents,
as if I were acquainted with all these people and would be
equally absorbed by the minute detail of their everyday lives. Her
girlfriend was secretly going out with a divorced man who had
two kids almost her age and he wanted to marry her her girlfriend's cousin who was older sixteen regularly sneaked out of her
house at night to go to a hotel with her boyfriend and sneaked
back before breakfast so that her parents never knew she was
gone the sons of close family friends turned out to be junkies and
she never knew it one of them was even a pusher she asked her
mother about birth control pills and was told that she would be
allowed to get them when she wanted them but was still considered
a bit too young her parents told her they wanted to be considered
her friends she told her parents she would rather consider them
her parents she didn't want to rebel because there was nothing to
rebel against she didn't want to conform because there was

nothing to conform to. And she was just like the crazy kids at
the college in that she had at bottom the same stubborn in-
difference about her future that I used to have about my past.

Yesterday I went to the dentist. I sat back in the chair as usual
while he stuck me with the novocaine. In a few minutes instead of
getting the normal numbjaw I begin feeling peculiar. Before I
know it I start shaking spastically, jerking and quivering all over
as if I were having an attack of epilepsy or St. Vitus's dance.
Seizures of leg trembling, body quaking, orgasmic back archings,
uncontrollable spasms. An idiosyncratic reaction to the novocaine, atypical and unpredictable. It went on and on I couldn't
stop. Meanwhile the dentist tipping my head back, taking my
pulse, applying smelling salts, swabbing me with alcohol, against
a creeping numbness and cold. For a few minutes there I thought
I could die. I once heard of such a case. When it was over I found
it had been going on for well over an hour. I couldn't believe it
I thought it had been maybe fifteen minutes. Shortly I felt okay
again, fine in fact, a little sleepy, a little like after an orgasm. I
got my teeth fixed and drove home. The thing is, how does this
fit in? That's it, it doesn't.

The rumor is that the government is going to make twenty
more arrests of resistance people within the next week. If so, let's
hope for some sign of public revulsion and general backlash
before they really begin to get heavy. As repression this is relatively nothing compared to what could happen. Maybe the
government is losing its cool. The only chance now is to keep
pushing them til they do. Everything else has proved futile. Then
hope for repression to backfire. A fundamental resistance tech-
nique. The velvet glove wears thin on the mailed fist. When power
is forced to increase its visibility it is that much closer to becoming
a target. But this can only be done by exposing oneself evidently.

> at least four times hit her with all
> his force then thrust his club
> swordlike between her hands into
> her face two more troops came up
> and began dragging the girl we
> could see her face but there was
> no face raw skin and blood her
> eyes had filled with the blood

pouring down her head she vom-
ited that too blood

I hear Canada has just made immigration more difficult.

Visitation from clear-eyed Athena, invisible, yet audible. Code
name for my agent. The crystal freshets of her voice, near, yet as
from a distance, were like the plashing of a mountain stream to
the thirsty traveler. A certain large circulation magazine loves my
novel but probably won't print any of it. Too outré. Will call
back with further news. Money running out. I have some hot job
leads. Absolutely essential to find some work soon. But careful
with that. No sooner had I written that into the end of my novel
than the telephone rang and I found some.

We now have a pair of black-capped chickadees with us.

Affair with fifteen-year-old, how carried on. Continuity in this
piece is like that in the daily comic strips. Phone calls were nerve
wracking. I had to call at certain times when she was most likely
to be there, her parents least likely. If one of her parents answered
it was agreed that I would give a name always beginning with J
since she didn't know anybody whose name began with J. Always
a different name dig, Jay, Joel, Jerry, Jack, and I would try to
change my voice a little each time, high or deep, slurred or clear,
slightly different accents. Deep voice: Good evening señora, thees
ees Juan, might I have the pleasure to speak with the señorita?
Vague mumble: Like is Teddy home man? Like this's Joey baby
know what I mean yeah. High pitched: Jawaharlal here. Likee
speakee Teddee. I kept lecturing her on the subject of discretion.
She'd already made a confidante of her younger sister, age twelve.
Also her house seemed to be full of telephone extensions. We'd be
involved in a long discussion about different kinds of contracep-
tion, or the advantages and disadvantages of young girls going
out with older married men, when I'd hear click, and after
another minute or so, click, and Teddy's voice yelling, I'm on the
phone. One day she started rehashing our latest experiments with
the sex act, and the phone started clicking like a pinball machine
gone wild. I imagine the following little scenario: Her mother
picks up the phone, discovers somebody's using it, and hangs up.
Then quickly does a double take, picks the phone up again,
listens for a minute, feels guilty about eavesdropping, and hangs
up again. Experiences countersurge of maternal rights and re-

sponsibilities, and picks up the phone. Unable to believe her ears she hangs up and calls her husband. He picks up the phone, listens for a few seconds, and hangs up out of embarrassment. He picks it up again out of curiosity. Hangs up again out of propriety. Picks it up again out of lasciviousness. Hangs up out of guilt. Picks up out of anger. Hangs up out of exasperation. Picks up and hands to wife, who glares, and hands it back. He shrugs and hangs up. They stare at one another. You better talk to Teddy, he says. She won't tell me anything, she says. I'll call the police, he says. Do that, she says. What about a private detective then? he says. How about mixing a couple of martinis? she says. I don't know, he says, I think I'd rather blow some pot. Maybe we better get her the pill after all, she says.

Don't talk about things like that over the phone, I tell Teddy when I see her. Don't worry, she says, my parents are hip. Besides, what can they do? If they bring you up on statutory rape I won't testify. She looked a lot like a tufted titmouse, which is a pretty, dark-eyed, round-breasted little bird, that hops around with a lot of quick head posturing, and has a lot of nerve for its size. If you know that wing panel from the Van Eyck Altarpiece of the Lamb devoted to the depiction of Eve, cover up the face, and you have a pretty good idea of what Teddy looked like without any clothes on. Very round breasts, a little baby fat around the middle, small hard ass, hard childish thighs all muscle. We were walking down Avenue B to my place. The whimsical West Indian wise guy who worked across the street watched us and wove me into some calypso verses which he'd be sure to sing to my wife. Regis nodded at me out of his whisky wisdom, aged over sixty years. The lady from upstairs who worked everything into an ongoing fantasy that involved people shooting at her, was muttering her own violent interpretations. The kid across the hall who is the same age and sex as Teddy blinked as we passed and went on playing with her yo-yo. This would be the first time we were alone together in private. I shoved my key into the lock.

Assuming language has been corrupted, said Neal, as I assume it has, why write anything? Why talk for that matter?

Why don't you shut up? I said.

No seriously, if what I said is true, said Neal, then the only attitude towards words is irony. And the end point of irony is silence. So why not save ourselves a lot of trouble and, like Babel, simply practice the art of silence?

In certain circumstances, I said, silence is a justifiable act of negation. In Babel, speaking of Babel, silence is capable of bringing the walls down.

That's my idea, said Neal. We've had too many words. We need action. Violence, subversion, anarchy, anything to destroy the system. You have to tear everything down in order to build it up. The only trouble is, that when you start destroying civilization, it seems, you have to be ready to destroy yourself.

That's a terrorist mentality, I told him. Before you know it you'll be planting plastiques or walking around with an infernal machine strapped to you like a character out of a Russian novel.

That's an appealing idea, he said.

Nothing is worth dying for, I told him. If you don't believe that then you believe in death. The only thing that will come out of that will be more death.

It appears that I can't live and I can't die then, he said. All I can do is drive fast.

Driving fast is an artificial situation.

Then give me a real one.

That you have to improvise.

That's asking too much.

I'm not asking anything. But let me point out for somebody who likes silence so much, you talk an awful lot. Why?

Because I can't shut up.

Right. I've noticed that people who talk about silence never commit it. There must be something they want that they're not getting. I wish I could figure out what.

I'm going for a drive, he said. I'll think about it.

No you won't, I said.

There are a lot of different ways of driving. Living in the country here I have to do everything by car. Driving to get somewhere is in itself merely utilitarian. Driving fast is in itself merely an exercise of power, and as such a flirtation with death. But driving so that you enjoy the motion, the control, the scenery, that's the only way to drive.

The alarm clock rang, and Joshua Jericho awoke in an immense, ornate, and downy-soft bed, of which he had no prior recollection. The quilt was decorated with gilt brocade that glanced and glinted in the sun like fields of golden-glancing-glinting wheat waving under the winking sun. And indeed its patchwork pattern resembled Kansas from a Boeing 707. The white cuff of the sheet disappeared in the distance on either side of him like the line of surf receding in a mist when seen from a seaside cliff. The pillow towered above him like the snows of Annapurna cradling in its skirts a tiny Sherpa village. The ceiling arched over him, a distant blue, with clouds and angels, like something by Tiepolo. The rich wall hangings stirred in a mild breeze produced by the strange musicks played by hidden musicians thrumming a light air appropriate to rising. Three beauteous young maids in flowing garb appeared, topless, to kiss him, stroke his penis, and rub his cheeks between their nipples, that the transition from sleep to waking might not be overly traumatic. In addition they rubbed his feet, brushed his teeth, cleaned out his nose holes, syringed his ears, and gave him an alcohol rub, back and front. A manservant appeared with rashers, citrons, melons, stacks of steaming pancakes dribbling with nuggets of melting butter, yolk-perfect eggs, oven-warm croissants, and pitchers of frothy *caffè làtte*. Joshua Jericho was washed and dressed and greased with precious oils and his every wish seemed to be telepathically intercepted, transmitted by radar to a computer, and swiftly administered by gracious courtiers, or glowing courtesans, as the case might be. He was then led out onto the terrace which overlooked the territory in order to observe his realms, that they might please him. Then came a lady stately and gracious, willowy and sinuous, dizzling and dazzling, and very pneumatic, and asked if Joshua Jericho would like to take his pleasure with her. Golly! said Joshua. Who are you? I know thee not. The lady disappeared. Then Joshua looked around and sweeping his arm toward the distance, said, and what are these realms? I know them not. And they disappeared. Joshua was left looking at, as it were, an empty canvas. Thus it was he turned and trod across the terrace, and reentered the chamber where he first awoke. What is this chamber? said Joshua. Who are these servants? I know them not. And they disappeared. And what is this break-fast, he said, that I have eaten? And Joshua was hungry. Joshua Jericho looked around. He was surrounded by, as it were, sheer nothingness, discouraging to behold. Thus it was that Joshua went back to bed, and covered himself with the mighty covers, and burrowed his head under the great pillow. And he muttered, What is this mighty bed in which I awoke? I know it not. And lo the bed disappeared, and Joshua was left floating, as it were, with nothing beneath him, and nothing above him, and nothing on either side of him, weightless, adrift in nothing, yet hurtling through the void all the while at the speed of light. Whereupon Joshua Jericho considered within himself for a moment, much discouraged, and downcast, and looking around him grumbled, What is this nothing? I know it not. And Joshua Jericho then turned of himself over on his side, and resting his head on his arm, went back to sleep. And then Joshua Jericho had a dream, and the dream was passing strange. And this was Joshua Jericho's dream. Joshua Jericho dreamed that the alarm clock rang, and that he awoke in an immense, ornate, downy-soft bed of which he had no prior recollection. And Joshua Jericho looked around him, and smiled, and knew it was a dream, and dreamed that he was happy.

UFO last night between five and six A.M. Lynn and I watched it in the sky over the hills for maybe half an hour. Distant bright yellow, vaguely star shaped, but possibly consisting of several lights, fewer on top than on bottom. Seemed to rotate in the air this way and that. Moved much faster than the stars, but more slowly than a man-made satellite would. Finally we went to sleep, it continued to wherever it was going. Live and let live I say.

Why don't we take a walk, I said.

Okay, she said.

We left the cafeteria and went outside to the campus, not saying much. I had trouble talking to Betty outside of class. She had the same trouble with me. I don't know why, maybe because she was always high, or because I wasn't.

One's body isn't private property, she repeated. It's a great feeling when you get rid of that idea. That's one reason why I got divorced. Do you ever feel that way?

I feel that way right now, I told her. She looked at me sideways.

Where are we going? she asked.

Good question, I asked. I thought we were taking a walk.

Well we seem to be walking all right, she said. She was turned on like I was turned on. I knew it and she knew it. All I had to do was touch her. I wanted to be quick while it lasted. Never let those moments go by. But where? My car was the only place I could think of, but it was parked right in the middle of campus. The hell, maybe it would last till I drove somewhere. I touched her hand, she slipped hers into mine. I glanced at her and she looked back with a look that meant no bullshit. We headed toward the car, not talking. We came to the car, I let her in one side and got in around the other. I put my arm around her shoulders.

Where to? I asked. She didn't answer but kind of sank against me. We traded a kiss, and she sort of kept sinking till her head hit my lap. I was caressing her hair, her body, her breasts. She curled up on the seat with her head in my lap. I took my coat off and put it over her. I pressed her face against my cock. She bit it and started unzipping my pants. I got my coat over her head. She was partly on the seat partly on the floor. I was rubbing my cock against her cheek, her lips, her eyelids. People were passing by, students I knew, teachers. I kept nodding seriously, as if I were preoccupied with some very important line of reasoning, the absentminded professor. At most it looked as if there were a bundle of something on the seat next to me, unless somebody got up too close. I started the motor in case I had to drive away fast. Actually she had my cock in her mouth and I wouldn't really have given a shit if the president of the college came over and started chatting about the weather. A colleague passed. I nodded and gave him an absent and probably very blissful looking smile. Star gazing? he shouted with a chuckle. Yeah, I yelled back, on the verge of an uncontrollable spasm. I came just after he passed, wondering whether anybody saw. She came up gulping and licking her lips. I sighed and said, Don't wipe your face. Oh I wouldn't do that she said, do you think I'm a prude? I gave her a quick peck on the cheek. I sighed again and smiled, and suddenly began laughing.

What are you laughing at? she asked.

I don't know, I said. I looked around. People were still passing by. We were right in the middle of campus. I kept laughing and laughing.

What's so funny? she asked.

Nothing, I said, I'm laughing because I'm happy.

Oh, she said.

I stepped on the gas and got out of there, still laughing. We drove a while.

Where we going? she asked. I shrugged.

Why don't we go to the city, she said. I know an apartment we can use on the East Side.

Okay, I said. New York was less than an hour's drive. I commuted a few days every week. We ended up in somebody's crash pad on Tenth west of A. We walked in and very cool she took off her clothes. Smiling, she lay down on a mattress on the floor and stared up at the ceiling.

I want a drink, I said. She made a face. She never touched alcohol.

There's nothing here, she said. There's some pot in the drawer. I rolled a joint and sat down next to her on the mattress and we smoked it while I caressed her. She stared at the ceiling. I was in a kind of pink revery of which her body was part. I went and pissed, came back, undressed, and lay down next to her. My cock was very impersonal, an animated hose with a life of its own, jumping around between her sensitive and very knowing fingers.

I think of you as Miss America, I said. She smiled. I slid in like a dirigible sliding into a cloud in a beautiful dream. Her body began churning like a bump and grind dancer. She was staring at the ceiling. Suddenly I got the feeling that this was all staged, some kind of routine, a movie maybe, or a cheap story. Her pussy felt like a moist sack of warm membrane, totally physiological. I had something like a sudden Hindenburg disaster. Shit, she said after a while. I flopped out, my penis a dead fish, my heart an empty reservoir.

Sorry, I said. I felt awful. The only time that had ever happened was with an old tank of a whore in London, 1959.

It doesn't matter, she said.

No?

It happens sometimes, she said.

Yeah, I said. Next time, I said. She smiled.

Any time, she said. We went to

An air of crisis pervades the household this morning. The roof is leaking like mad from the thawing snow, the garage doors are cracked and hanging from the abrasion of the ice on the ground, and we are being overrun by field mice. Every time you set a trap you get another dead mouse, with an inexhaustible supply scampering around the house. I hate to kill them, they're sort of cute. Unlike city mice. Except they shit all over everything, and frighten Lynn, who, as a form of exorcism, mimics them and keeps giving them names: Blacky, Whiskers, Pinky, Alice. Oh well, they're better than the rats on Avenue B.

Right this minute there's a downy woodpecker, male, outside the window pecking at the trunk that I rubbed the suet on. Now here's a blacked capped chickadee. And here's an incredibly fat and beautiful cardinal, blinding red, with dark modulations on top, cocking his head inquisitively like an intellectual. This is the longest period of time we've been up here, two weeks. Sunday back to Avenue B. This is Friday. By then this performance will be finished. I'll be glad for the change. I go back to the city like a sailor on shore leave, or like a monk coming out of retreat. Back to the world with its business and its adventures.

Lynn says she'll be in my story soon, but is getting impatient because, as she points out, she has her own interests. Isn't that a quote from my novel?

I just cleaned the snow off the roof and disposed of Pinky and Alice. That leaves Whiskers and Frank Budgen.

We went to sleep. I had a dream of Betty as a housewife. I had come to read her meter but I couldn't find it, and I had the feeling that she was concealing it from me. She kept asking me for "cigs" and gave me an American cheese sandwich on white bread with a lot of mayonnaise. I woke up with an erection. I caressed Betty awake. She felt it and moaned. I stuck it between her legs. Suddenly it wriggled and went limp like a punctured balloon. I tried to stuff it in with my fingers, but it was like stuffing toothpaste back into the tube. I decided it was time to go.

Now the point is, Lynn, whether you mind my having all these, what?

Do you have to say my name?

Of course. Whether you mind my having all these girlfriends in my stories.

How many?

How many where?

Girlfriends.

Well, in general, I mean, wait a minute. Since this is a story you have to say "she said" after everything you say.

Do I really?

Yes. Because how are people going to tell, right?

Oh I don't like that.

She said.

I don't like that.

She said.

Because that's like living at a distance from your own body.
She said.

That's like the character in "A Painful Case" in *Dubliners*.
What's that? She said I mean I said.

Everything he thought he appended a pronoun and a verb in
the past tense, to every thought.

For example.

Well he would think, um, "The world works in mysterious
ways, he said."

Oh, really? I said. Would you rather I said I said, since I'm
writing the story I'll say, okay since I'm writing the story I'll say
I said. And she said.

Fine. I'm your character. Except for the dialogue.

Okay. So, all right? let's get back to what I wanted to know is
whether you had, whether you minded, whether you mind my
having all these girls in my stories.

No I think it's nice that they're in your stories.

There are two in this story.

Are they one dark and one fair.

More or less, yes.

Like chocolate and marshmallow?

Uh, she said. That's not, that's not their names, I said.

Are they very young?

One is. Very young. I said.

Oh but one is older?

One is somewhat older, I said.

How old?

She said. Which, which? Well one is fifteen. I said.

How old is the other one?

And the other is about twenty-one.

Oh.

She said. But you're also in the story. I said.

What do I do?

She said. You talk like you're talking now. I said. And also you occupy the place where the story is being composed, namely here, and are referred to as for example in your naming of the mice, I said.

Is this now to find out whether I'm jealous?

She said.

That is, do you, am I a jealous character who is now going to either live or unlive her jealousy in your story?

She said. Well that depends completely on you, I said. I never brought up . . .

Can I talk about something different and not about these girls who I don't care about, the little snips?

She said. Okay, I said. What would you like to talk about, I said.

Daniel Deronda.

I think I'm going to end this now. I said. All right, would you like to talk about *Daniel Deronda?*

No I wouldn't really but that's what's on my mind because I'm a I'm a scholar at the moment.

She said.

I'll try to think myself back into womanliness, and have an attitude. Why do you want, why do you have them of those ages, what entices you about those ages, why don't you have two fifteen-year-olds, or one thirty-five-year-old and one ten-year-old?

She said. Well I don't know, uh, because they just happen to be uh, they just happen to come up, I said.

Do you like them equally well?

Oh, I don't really like them, I said. I mean, really like them. After all they're only characters, I said.

But you as a character do you as a character really like them well?

She said. Well, yeah, I'm sort of fond of them. I said.

Well then I am too. Why don't we all go to the movies together?

All right, what would you like to see? *Jules and Jim* perhaps? I said.

Le Bonheur.

Le Bonheur. She said, I mean he said. He repeated.

Your fangs are gleaming.

She said. You know, we only have twenty more.

Twenty more what?

You only have a hundred. I said. She said.

A hundred what? Will you stop these stupid he says, we could get more in.

A hundred things on the recorder. I mean twenty, twenty more. I said.

Do you do lecherous things with these girls in the story?

No. I just fuck them. I said.

That's what I mean.

Well, then I guess I do. I said.

Separately or together as in your novel, *Up?*

Uh, separately, I said. Would you like to think of a witty and appropriate remark in conclusion I said, I asked?

Certainly not. She said.

Thank you, I said.

I turned off the recorder. This is going to be one of the best parts of my story, I said.

Great, she said. Now will you come up and write a page of my paper?

Becoming real again, she returns to, as she puts it, her own interests. What I need is a bunch of friends who would be willing to become my characters for a whole story. Maybe I can hire some. Somebody ought to start a character rental service. I suppose that's what actors are. In a way. But then they don't participate in the composition of their own stories. What I'd really like is the comments of my models on their characterizations, but this is in most cases difficult to obtain.

Once upon a time, Junior Junior, Jr., known to his friends simply as Junior, was walking down the street when, happening to pass by a newsstand, and looking at a paper, he discovered that it wasn't that time at all, but the day before. This was strange, for Junior could remember exactly what had happened the day before, including what was in the newspapers. Assuming a case of massive *déjà vu*, Junior decided to ignore yesterday, and went on acting as if it were tomorrow. Thus he went to the office, and did tomorrow's work, completely neglecting today's, which he had already done. At lunch time, Junior's boss commended him for having done so much of tomorrow's work, but censured him for completely neglecting today's. I'll do it yesterday, said Junior. You are confused, said his boss. It occurred to Junior that he was, since tomorrow was Saturday, and he shouldn't be at the office at all if today was tomorrow. And if today was yesterday, he'd already done his work, and therefore there was no reason for him to be here anyway. So Junior left his office, and didn't come back, neither that day, nor the next, since he didn't know when that was, nor the next, nor the next. This, then, is how Junior went out one morning and lost all his days, and explains why ever since he has been wandering in a limbo between yesterday and tomorrow, never knowing whether to do a thing, or not to do it. For if he went to do a thing, he never knew whether he had already done it, or whether he should refrain from doing it since he was supposed to do it tomorrow. He could neither do what he had done yesterday, nor what he was supposed to do tomorrow. Junior was definitely out of step. And this is what saved Junior, for finally he decided to forget all about yesterday and tomorrow, since he could do nothing with them. From then on when Junior walked down the street and passed a newsstand it was always today. Every day was today, no matter what day it was. Yesterday was today, tomorrow was today. Junior really began to enjoy himself. He would wake up today, and look forward with pleasure to a day of things that had never happened before, and would never happen again. He would go through the day with gusto and vivacity. But soon things began to turn sour. Junior began to lose all his friends, for example. For one thing he had great difficulty keeping appointments made for some day in the future, because there was no day in the future. For another, Junior knew nothing of the joys of common memory which we all share. If one of his friends brought up something they had done together in the past, Junior would simply look puzzled and say, But that was today. It was all one long today for Junior. He had neither nostalgia nor anticipation, neither regret nor dread. Soon Junior found himself completely isolated. You could see him any day, say, today, walking down the street looking innocent and bemused. People would nod to one another knowingly and tap their heads when he passed. There goes Junior, they would say, he thinks it's today. Junior languished and withered. He was already dead to the world, and the world dead to him, entombed in today. When he actually died, he died, unlike other people, on a day on which he had never died before, and on which he would never die again. On, in fact, today. His tombstone bears the following inscription: *Junior Junior, Jr. Age 35. Born today. Lived today. Died today.*

I shoved the key into the lock, and felt the mechanism inside respond as I turned it and opened the door. I relieved her of her coat and her briefcase full of school books, which weighed a ton. I was glad that Lynn had left the apartment neat. I wanted the transition from Central Park East to Avenue B as untraumatic as possible. I kept my fingers crossed that no water bugs would appear on the scene. I made some tea for us and, nervously chewing a toothpick, sat down on the couch next to her.

Can I have a toothpick? she asked. I gave her a toothpick. After a while we started making out. At a certain point I told her to take her clothes off.

Do I have to? she asked.

No you don't have to, I said. You don't have to do anything. Only what are you doing here?

Visiting for tea? she asked.

Look, this isn't Park Avenue. I put my arm around her semi-paternally, which was an easy thing to fall into when in physical contact because her youth was emphasized by her littleness.

If you want to go on being a virgin, I said, it's okay with me. I had a sudden traumatic memory of desperate coaxing scenes from my own adolescence.

I'm not a virgin, she said with quiet defiance.

You're not, I thought you were.

Oh no, she said.

Since when? I asked.

Since I was thirteen. It was my fourteenth birthday really when it happened, she corrected herself.

How did it happen? I asked.

My boyfriend, she said. He was older.

How old? I asked.

Sixteen. We went to his house after my birthday party. His parents were out. He used Baggies for contraceptives.

We laughed.

Very sentimental, I said.

Oh it was. He was a nice boy. I liked him. But I stopped going out with him after that because I didn't want to keep making love with him.

Was that the end of your lovemaking experience?

No. There was a college boy over the summer. But he's away now. Besides that's over. Are you surprised?

Yeah, but I'm all for it.

I undressed her. She was passive. Her pussy was narrow and unyielding till suddenly she got excited, and it expanded like a balloon inflating. I forgot her age until afterwards, when she asked whether everything was all right.

Terrific, I said. She smiled abruptly, but after that she was very cool. More cool than I knew she was. I had an image of one of those people on a ship during a storm who, though green and trembling, refuses to admit that the ride is rough for fear of immediately getting sick. Then I knew that she would refuse to admit the existence of anything that was happening to her which she could not understand, handle, or do something about, and remembering myself, knew again what it was like to be that young. She would go to pieces if forced to confront her own helplessness, and so her cool was a way of protecting herself from that experience she wanted so badly because it would ultimately make her more autonomous, would free her from her ignorance. From that point on I was no longer free to treat her as an equal, yet I continued to do so, out of inertia or, more likely, because I was unwilling to invest myself in anything so complicated as becoming a combined teacher-therapist-parent. We had a nice, comradely hour in a taxi caught in a traffic jam while I was taking her home.

At about this time Neal told me that he was giving up his 2A deferment, which was, he added, his only remaining reason for being in graduate school. So I guess I'll be getting out of here pretty soon too, he said.

Dog-tongue Mike, who was having coffee with us, clapped him on the shoulder. That's groovy man, that's the thing to do. That's real gutsy, he said, panting with enthusiasm.

If it's so great why don't you do it, asked Neal.

Mike shrugged. I don't wanna go to jail. When I go to jail it's gotta be over something really worth it. Like clobbering one of the FBI guys they got crawling around this campus.

It is the gutsy thing to do all right, I said. I was very suspicious of anything Neal did that looked self-destructive. Why do you feel obliged to go to jail? I asked.

Nothing is real, said Neal. Maybe jail will be real.

Jesus, if jail is the only thing that's real . . .

I might as well kill myself, right? said Neal. No there are a few other things that are real. Clobbering an FBI agent would be real.

Violence is about the only thing left that's real, said Mike, panting hard. Wait till the next demonstration man. Everybody's tired of laying around and getting his head beat in.

You guys will end up killing somebody. Or getting killed.

Assassinating somebody is more like it, said Neal. That's the only thing that's gonna do any good.

You're lapsing into fantasy.

The Kennedy assassination was a fantasy too, said Neal. I know it was because I saw it on television. I would kill the President if I could. It would be the most meaningful thing I could do with my life.

I'll take care of Humphrey, said Mike, panting.

Who's gonna get McCormack? I said. You wouldn't wanna be stuck with McCormack, would you? You see what I mean? Where does it end?

I don't know where it ends, said Neal. I just wanna see it begin. Because I'm totally sick of the way it is. I've really had it up to here.

You know this conversation is being taped, I said. They've installed a microphone in my bridgework.

Yeah I can believe it, said Neal. What do they expect to pick up that way?

I don't know, I said. They get a lot of gurgle.

You guys aren't getting paranoid are you? said Mike.

Who's paranoid? said Neal. We will now have a chorus of God Bless Amurica.

I decided it was time to go. I told Betty I had to get back. She sat up on the mattress.

You don't have to go you know, she said.

I know.

Don't feel bad, she said.

I feel wonderful. It was a gas. We'll try again sometime soon.

Whenever you're ready, she said, just wink, or blink, or whistle, or whatever it is you do.

That night was the beginning of my new schedule. I got home about three A.M. Lynn was asleep. I worked through till next afternoon, until I had to drive out and give my class, and then came home and went to sleep. After that I went to sleep whenever there was a convenient spot in the day. Every now and then I'd forget whether it was day or night for a minute, or lose a whole day of the week without being able to figure it out. I'd go out to teach, and I'd see Betty, who would keep glancing at me expect-antly, then maybe I'd race in to the city to see Teddy on her way home from school, and get home in time for dinner with Lynn, work on my two books all night, and prepare for class in the morning. I started calling Betty Teddy and Teddy Betty. One time Teddy called while Betty was there. She answered the phone and handed it to me with a suspicious look. By the time I got to the phone I couldn't figure out who the hell it was I was talking to. Another time I met a colleague who assumed Teddy was my daughter. Afraid he would find out I didn't have a daughter, I told him she was my wife. In his fluster he forgot my name when introducing us to his wife, and at that point I couldn't think of it either, so I gave the name of another colleague and hoped none of us would ever meet again. The compartments of my personality were beginning to break down. At times I would forget where I was. I'd suddenly start talking like a professor while drinking with my friends, or like a hippie while teaching my class. I got through everything in a kind of frenzy, working out a frantic death rhythm that I couldn't seem to escape. Nobody ever realized that I was out of step, for the very good reason that I wasn't.

Robbe-Grillet's insistence on the self-destroying form, I was saying, like that of certain artists, Tinguely for example, is a denial of any *a priori* order, and at the same time an assertion of freedom. One could apply the same idea to the problematic con-cept of personal identity as in, say, the novels of Beckett. As I talked, Betty was rubbing her thigh against my knee under the seminar table. Freedom in this context can mean only one thing, the freedom to create, and to create continuously, out of the fragmented, contradictory, anomalous, and progressively dis-sociating elements of our experience, a life that is coherent as a work of art is coherent, that continually comes together as it continuously comes apart. Betty kept rubbing her thigh against me as I was talking. The more she rubbed the faster I talked. I was getting an enormous erection.

Here begins the last hour that I allow myself to finish this performance. Go.

When the class was over I turned to her and told her I'd like to see her in my office. She followed me down the hall. I let her in and locked the door. I pushed her up against the desk. Lie

down, I said. She arched back on her elbows, toes pressing
against the floor. I peeled her jeans off and unzipped my fly. She
was lying on my desk in her panties. I pulled them off. I felt like
a cannon. She wrapped her thighs around my waist as I aimed
and cocked. I plunged. Fucking thing collapsed like a telescope.
I cursed. Get dressed, I told her. Stay cool, she said. I cursed
again, zipped up, and raged out of the office slamming the door
behind me. Stay cool, she was urging as I left, some other time.
If I were her I would have been angry as hell. The girl was
absolutely selfless. She was like an empty hole.

Go on.

I can't.

Keep going.

This is the story of Jimmy the Jay, and how he got his name.
Once there was a Jay, and he flew around the fields looking for
something to eat. But this Jay, instead of pecking for seeds, or
worms, or insects, like the other birds, had a different way of
finding things to eat. He would fly up to another bird's nest, and
the mother bird, or the father, or one of the baby birds if the
parents were out, would peer up over the side of the nest and say,
Who are you? And the Jay would say, Gimme! Gimme! Gimme!
And then he would peck away, and take whatever was in the nest,
while the other birds flew around scolding frantically. Gimme!
Gimme! Gimme! And he'd steal the seeds that were there, or the
worms, or even the eggs of the unhatched baby birds. Again and
again the Jay would fly up to a nest, and the residents would ask,
Who are you? What do you want? And he'd say, Gimme! Gimme!
Gimme! and take whatever was in the nest. Thus passed the
spring, and the summer and the fall, and in the winter, when
everything had sort of quieted down in the country, and the baby
birds were all grown up some so they could start getting their
education, all the birds began to tell stories about this Jay who
would go around robbing everybody's nest. And they traded
stories, and they warned one another, and pretty soon, one wise
old crow wrote the whole thing down, so that everybody would
know about this Jay, and would know to look out for him. So the
crow recorded the story of the robber Jay and his terrible ex-
ploits. And his manuscript was passed around the bird circuit.
And it was mostly the little birds who got to read it because the

older birds were out foraging for what little food there was during the winter and it was only the little birds who had a chance to read. But a lot of the little birds couldn't read too well because they were just beginning. And so, instead of reading "Gimme! Gimme! Gimme!" for the Jay's cry, they would read "Jimmy! Jimmy! Jimmy!" And so they got to thinking that the Jay's name must be Jimmy. Now when the spring came, and the Jay started going around again trying to rob everybody's nest, and the big birds were out looking for food, and the little birds, who had just started flying practice, were the only ones around the nest, and the Jay would fly up, the little birds would all say, Who are you? And the Jay would say, Gimme! Gimme! Gimme! And the little birds would look at one another, and they would say to one another, He must mean Jimmy. He must have a speech defect. And pretty soon, every time the Jay would come up to a nest, the little birds would say, Hey, it's Jimmy, Jimmy. And after a while the Jay got to know his name. That's me, he thought, I'm Jimmy. And he would fly up to a nest, and everything would be completely different, because the birds would say, Hi Jimmy. And the Jay would say, Hi folks. And the birds in a very neighborly way would begin to offer Jimmy some of whatever little food they happened to have around, And Jimmy was really touched by this because he was really a good bird at heart, and after a while he would go around helping to find food for the birds who didn't have enough. And pretty soon, when Jimmy flew up to a nest, all the other birds knew that it was a friend, and Jimmy couldn't do much else but be friendly. And the wise old crow nodded, as if he knew what was going to happen all along, and he wrote it all down, and this story is the story he wrote.

Faster.

Teddy began to show up late for appointments. She would get to my place late, and at first I was very cool. On top of that it was getting sticky arranging to have my apartment free so that I found myself making out with her in nerve-wracking unlikely places, like St. Patrick's Cathedral and the Cloisters.

Keep going.

I was sitting with Neal in the cafeteria. The hip types were at the next table playing their games.

Go on. Faster.

I was getting really sick of kids. Betty at about this time had pretty much dropped out of school and drifted into the Lower East Side.

Keep it up. Faster.

Clark Clifford a friend and intimate advisor to President Johnson was appointed Secretary of Defense to succeed Robert McNamara who will leave the post on March 1 Mr. Clifford has consistently supported every aspect of the President's Viet Nam policy except the bombing pauses

the administration is trying to conceal its political ineptitude with military strength in Viet Nam Senator George D. Aiken charged we are fighting nationalists first in Viet Nam said the Vermont Republican who is the second ranking minority member of the Foreign Relations Committee

there are also a lot of nice buildings in Haiphong what their contributions are to the war effort I don't know but the desire to bomb a virgin building is terrific I was fascinated with the Navy and flying since I was a kid he went on I was always a big fan of Charles Lindbergh and I saw Dawn Patrol with Errol Flynn at least eight times

302,000 men face draft in '68 a 72,000 increase

four men with afro-style hair cuts and black muslim crescent symbols on gold chains entered a Brooklyn junior high school complained to the principal that pupils had allegedly been locked

out during last week's freezing
weather then beat the principal
and two school officials
at least four times hit her with
all his force then thrust his club
swordlike between her hands into
her face two more troops came up
and began dragging the girl we
could see her face but there was
no face raw skin and blood her
eyes had filled with the blood
pouring down her head she vom-
ited that too blood

I was in Tompkins Square Park listening to some live music
from the bandshell when a hip-rock group came on and started
playing. Right away the Puerto Ricans in the crowd clutched their
heads and started yelling bloody murder. Wha kina noise's this?
They call this music? Pretty soon a few bottles hit the stage. Local
conga drums struck up a loud counterpoint. The kids pulled up
several oil drums and started pounding on them with sticks to
drown out the musicians. Firecrackers were going off all over the
place. The kids were climbing up onto the stage. The attendants
lowered the metal grate. The kids, monkey-like, climbed up the
grate and harassed the band. There wasn't a cop in sight. Finally
the group gave up and stopped playing. I saw them fighting their
way out the back of the bandshell through crowds of razzing
teenagers. Huge crowds of kids were racing unpredictably from
one side of the park to the other like flocks of nervous pigeons.
Firecrackers and cherry bombs were going off like guerilla war-
fare. I knew it was gonna blow sky-high and I started edging the
hell out of the park. Suddenly there was a tall blond on the hill in
the middle of the park in the center of a milling crowd. My
impression was that she was wearing something white and flowing.
I say my impression because the next minute she was nude to the
waist, clutching a rag of whatever it was she was wearing to her
breasts, and then that too was ripped away. She stood there her
arms over her breasts, the crowd pawing at her. Somebody pulled
her arms behind her back. A hand clamped her breast, was pulled
off, another hand grabbed her other breast. Hands were going up
under her skirt, part of the skirt came off, and then the rest was

torn away. Through all this the girl was silent, staring wide-eyed over the crowd. Her arms were pinned behind her and suddenly she was lifted up into the air in her panties and carried that way at a run across the park toward Avenue B at the head of a streaming mob. Kids tore past me on bikes saying, Hully jeez, hully jeez. They stopped in the middle of Avenue B, a mob filling the intersection and a block each way, still no cops, the girl lying in the street nude swallowed up in the center. A small kid was working his way through the crowd. I was lookin right up her chubbies, he said. Suddenly after a long, long time, a cop car was in the crowd, trying to make its way through to the center. Everybody surged around it rocking it back and forth, banging on the windows. A kid shouldered past me shouting, These chicks come round here to play their games man, this our turf. More patrol cars came screaming up and were stopped by the crowd. A Tactical Patrol van pulled into one of the side streets. The cops piled out and got into formation. People were climbing over cars, wrecking them, throwing rocks, bottles, garbage at the cops. A fleet of patrol cars began wailing down one street, a wedge of the Tactical Patrol charged up another. Everyone began running. I was caught in a stampede racing down the middle of Avenue B. I stopped two blocks away and began moving back toward the park. Bottles and garbage were coming down from the roofs. I saw a dead pigeon tossed from a rooftop and flop into the middle of the crowd. I was caught in another wave of people tearing down the Avenue. I got to the shelter of a doorway as people raced past. There were three guys in there already. See that, said a guy pointing to a car with its roof crushed in. That's my car. I can't even get to it, he said resignedly. Two guys were passing a bottle back and forth. Have a drink, one said. I took a gulp. Some scene, huh? said the guy with the bottle. The wise guy West Indian from the store across the street passed by at a trot and waved gleefully. I got back into the street and found myself running up the Avenue toward the park. Blazer appeared. Hey man, this is a kerazy scene, he said. Yeah, I said. He laughed, Man I'm really diggin it. I lost sight of him. Things were quiet for a while. I had a long conversation with a guy I never saw before about the corruption of the local cops. He started pointing out the plainclothesmen in the crowd. A lady from upstairs in my building came over to say hello. Ain it awful? she said. Her eyes were gleaming. The crowd started coming down the Avenue again. Everybody scattered, then ran back in the direction they just came from. Now the Tactical Patrol cops were moving down the sidewalks in two columns like an occupying army. They staked out the street corners, they sent men up to the rooftops, closing off the Avenue block by block and pushing the crowd in front of them. But it was like trying to block off an ocean. The crowd was behind them, surging into the park again. I saw a guy with blood pouring down his face being pulled away with his arms around the shoulders of two friends. And then suddenly, marching down the middle of the Avenue, rags and crutches, battered horn broken drum and kazoo like Yankee Doodle Dandy, two string guitar, bongo, ash-can tops, comb in tissue paper, back slapping, bottle swinging, the Kallikak band, with its crazy, tuneless, beatless, braying, musicless music.

Keep going.

Teddy showed up an hour late. Life was getting a little nerve-wracking at about this time. I hadn't gotten much sleep, I was falling behind on my books.

Where've you been? I asked her.

I had to see one of my teachers, she told me. I looked at my watch. There was about half an hour left before Lynn would be coming home.

Okay, take off your clothes, I told her.

Do I have to? she asked.

No you don't have to, I said, you don't have to do anything. But then what are you doing here?

She started getting undressed. I helped. I was a little sore this time. We started making out. Then she said, I don't want to make love today.

Then why did you start it? I asked.

I have my period, she said.

You don't have your period. I knew she didn't have her period. Come on, I said, what is it?

Nothing, she said.

You've been seeing somebody else today.

She didn't answer. I started trying to make out with her again.

I've just been making love, she said.

I'm getting sick of this, I said.

I suppose you want me to go now? she asked. She looked very stiff, I could see she was frightened.

That's right, I said. What really got me sore was that she seemed to assume she was privileged to break a date with me to go screw someone else or whatever the hell else she wanted to do and waste all my goddam time. I was sick of handling her with kid gloves. I was sick of kids. She was just a rich, spoiled, uptown brat, that's all there was to it.

She had her clothes on, she picked up her pocketbook and her briefcase full of books, and went to the door. I didn't say anything. She turned.

Look, she said, I can explain if . . .

I don't want any explanations, I said. I opened the door for her. She smiled a last-ditch reconciliation scene smile.

It was nice, I said, while it lasted. I shut the door and locked it. I still sweat when I think of that moment.

Keep going.

I was sitting with Neal in the cafeteria. The hip types were at the next table playing their games. The latest thing was shooting craps.

I got my 1-A, said Neal.

What are you gonna do? I asked.

Don't know. Not thinking about it.

How about going to Canada?

What's the point? I mean sooner or later somebody's gonna drop the bomb and that'll be it.

Ah come on. I thought you were going to jail.

When the time comes I'll think about it.

What are you doing tomorrow? Next month?

Why think about the future?

Are you counting on the apocalypse?

I'm not counting on anything. Everything's gonna blow sky-high pretty soon so what's the difference? You can feel it. It's already starting. Just pick up a newspaper.

That's just wishful thinking.

If it's going to start let it start. What are your plans?

I shrugged.

He opened his briefcase, took out a couple of comic books. He handed me a Superman. We sat around reading.

Go on. Faster.

Betty at about this time had pretty much dropped out of school and drifted into the Lower East Side. She was living with a pusher known as Tony the Roach and was involved with the fringes of a local sex cult about which, however, she was very condescending. She was beginning to be mentioned in the *Village Voice* in the "Scenes" column. Anyway around then I met her one day in Tompkins Square. We got to talking. It turned out she was doing a go-go bit at a hip discotheque. I do it topless sometimes, she said very casually, but only for private dances.

What's that like? I asked.

Why don't you come over to my place sometime. I'll show you. I called her that night. Come on over, she said, I'm alone.

I raced over and knocked at the door. I heard about seven locks unlock. The door opened, she was stark naked.

Oh, it's you, she said. I didn't say a word. I pressed her against me and started squeezing her buttocks, stuffing my fingers up her cunt. Somehow we landed on the bed. She was squirming under me. Suddenly she pushed me off and got up.

No, she said. Not again. I've had it. Want a joint? Tony even has some whisky here if you want.

I lay still on the bed, my fly open like a gaping mouth with its tongue hanging out. She went and poured me a drink. Bourbon? she asked, handing me the glass. I leaned on my elbow and gulped it down. She sat down next to me and started fiddling with my penis.

Too bad we can't make it, she said. It would've been nice.

I put the glass down. Cut the bullshit, I said. I grabbed her around the neck and pulled her down. She fought me off, she was pretty strong. We fell with a hard thump onto the floor. She was under me still fighting. I pried her legs open with my knee and pinned her arms behind her. Once I was in her she stopped fighting. She lay passive with her arms stretched back behind her head. It was going to be good. Slowly, she began responding, cooperating, urging me on. We were on the point of mutual orgasm when I heard the seven locks unlocking and, looking up, I saw this guy watching us, an enormous, black, Great Dane by his side.

I dint meet yiz, said the guy.

Oh, hi Tony, she said with a little laugh.

Go ahead, do your thing, he said. He went into the next room. Don't stop, she said. The Great Dane sniffed at my ass. I had a brief minor ejaculation, like the death spasm of a worm and fell out. Shit, she said.

I got up and zipped my pants. She was still lying naked on the floor. The Great Dane nosed her crotch. She pushed it away and sat up. Tony came back in.

Is this business or pleasure? he asked her.

Neither, she said.

Have a joint, Tony said. I took it and he lit it for me. He was a little bullnecked guy with five-o'clock shadow, low boots, pegged pants, a Second Avenue shirt with beads around his neck, and a kind of dark, seedy good-looks like an actor playing a gangster part, looked about twenty-five.

This is Tony, she said. He squatted on the floor and we passed the joint around.

Did yiz see the shit in the closet? he asked.

No, I don't think I did, she said.

This fucking monster shits on everything. It's too much. I hate it.

Why don't you get rid of it? I asked.

He smiled. He had an oddly boyish smile. Say it's necessary precautions. He looked at Betty angrily. Shit, he said, go put somethin on. Aincha got no morals?

She sighed with mock resignation, got up, and went into the next room. He smiled at me. These college girls, he said.

She came back dressed in sweater and jeans. Listen I got a job ya gotta do for me.

Oh. Am I working for you?

Ya gotta do this. He handed her a shoe box and mentioned an address. There's a friend a mine there, you'll see him. He's a jig.

Where were you? she asked.

I had a little business at the Ninth Precinct.

She nodded at me with genteel irony. Tony's taking over the neighborhood, she said.

He smiled. Yiz might say so.

What's in the box? she asked.

A gun.

What do you think I am, she said.

He smiled at me. I decided it was time to leave. Last I heard about Betty she'd left the city and he was looking to kill her.

Faster. Good angel milk. I was drinking good angel milk. I was sitting in the room of my good angel, we'll call her Angel, drinking good angel milk. She had walked out of an institution into my class, she was becoming a brilliant poet. She was teaching me how to drink good angel milk, that is she was my good angel and was teaching me how to sit still and drink milk. I kept bumming cigarettes from her and as I lit them and smoked them down kept drinking milk. We were listening to rock 'n' roll, The Doors: *All the children are insane/ waiting for the summer rain.*

I don't really dig that music, I told her. I didn't then.

Phone call. All my jobs for next year seem to have fallen through. Back to Avenue B.

I was drinking angel milk, good angel milk, smoking cigarettes and listening to The Doors. She looked like a cherub, or maybe a grown-up angel out of a Florentine painting, Fra Angelico, say. *All the children are insane/ waiting for the summer rain.*

I don't dig that music, I said. I just don't seem to have any feelings about it. It doesn't mean anything to me.

Well, she said, I guess if you don't have any feelings about it it's not going to have any meaning to you.

What?

I mean if you have a feeling for something then I guess it means something to you.

That was the moment when I started liking rock 'n' roll. And I still do. *Waiting for the summer rain.*

More milk? she asked.

Another call. And still another. Three calls in succession all pointing to financial catastrophe. This is what happens when you try to finish a story you been working on for two weeks in one hour. Nobody ever calls me here. Few people know my number. I set myself the hour, I start composing, and there you are. All plans shattered. Fuck it. I think I'll have a drink. I mean another drink. Angel milk. Everything's blowing up, falling to pieces. Art dissolves back into life. Chaos. It's not the way I planned it. Just burned my desk badly with a cigarette. What else can happen? The house can burn down. Finish my half pint, Golden Days. A little Jimmy Reed on the phonograph. I'm at my best when everything explodes. I thrive on chaos. I have a feeling for it, a blues mentality, if you know what I mean. I have a feeling for it. Actually I'm quite happy. Didn't wanna work next year anyway, not really. What a relief. And the review of my Stevens book, just got a good review in *The New York Review* one of the calls told me. That was one of the two books I was working on. Did anybody ever write a story like this? *I wanna roll you baby/ roll you all over town.* This isn't a story man, this is life. *Let me roll with you baby/ roll all over town.* Unfortunately it'll never be published. *Some time you have to cry/ some time you have to lie/ you can make it if you try.* But I'm not even gonna try, fuck it, I'm just gonna sit here and finish my half pint. *Feelin lowdown.* I knew I should never have gone for the interview on New Year's Day with that terrible hangover. Well that's the story of my life man. I'm a crow sitting on a fence, a crow who thinks he can keep his balance, and when I get pushed off onto the wrong side I start squawking, without once admitting that's the side I like best. All these years of experience and traditional painstaking methods plus modern scientific controls add up to that perfect combination of full-flavored whisky with the distilled-in mellowness. This whisky is at least six weeks old.

Enough. Saturday, January 20, 1968. Let's take a walk. I put on my boots. I walk out the door. The thaw is on. I walk through slush, melting ice and snow. I walk down the road. To the right the house, above a mountain, to the left a still snowy field. The chickadees are at the suet in the tree outside the study. We now have three chickadees. The chickadee is one sweet bird, I love those chickadees. It's almost fifty degrees, the sky is blue, I pass the stand of pines, I pass the mailbox, the cows down the road, the red, rumpled ones, will be out for the first time since the freeze began, the sun is already hitting the mountain behind the house, a few washy clouds begin to turn pink, Lynn is back in the house finishing her paper and doing her collages, I pass the red house at the curve, the one where nobody hardly ever is, a flock of slate-colored juncos chirp at me from a tree, last couple of days I've noticed one with an all white tail should I write the Audubon Society or what, a cardinal crimson against the snow, the dog down the road runs up tail wagging, he jumps up on me and I scratch behind his ear, scritch scritch scritch, his way of saying hello. The bottle is empty on my desk. That whisky smelled like paint remover. Where am I headed, don't know. I keep walking down the road. The sun begins to dip behind the mountain, I call it a mountain. A squirrel poses on the snowbank at the side of the road, maybe that bastard who's been at the birdseed. I aim a snowball at it and miss, it races up a tree. In the distance to the left down a side road or that is a side road to this side road, a long farmhouse with barn attached. And here's the bend in the road. I start around it. In a minute I'll be out of sight. But before I disappear, I lift my red wool cap that I bought so the hunters won't blow my head off, a gesture of goodbye, as if to say, in fact to say, I'm happy folks, and I wish you luck. I disappear around the bend.

So long. End of story.

ROAST BEEF : A SLICE OF LIFE

In the foreground the sounds of silver on crockery are more or less constant—in the background, those of voices, Latin music, trucks, buses.

HE	SHE
Okay you ready?	Mmhm. What's that?
Microphone.	
	I'm having V8 juice.
You're not gonna have wine? Ah Lynn then I'm not gonna have it.	No.
	Well I'm gonna have it in a wine glass to be effective but if I have wine I'm gonna feel ill.
What?	Well that's up to you. It's up to you but I really can't have any.
All right then I won't have any either.	You want some juice?
Can I have a glass?	

Sounds of water running, crockery, silver.

A toilet flushes. A door squeaks open.

I'm gonna have wine.	Okay. Do you think gentian violet goes down with the to- mato juice?

It doesn't matter. They put it
in babies' mouths.   They do?
Yeah.

You'll have to open it.   Me?
Yeah.   I don't know how.

You can just do the pulling
part.   Okay.
                                       Is this right so far?
Yeah. I'll screw it in.
                                       The other kind is better.
What other kind?   The other brand.
Here, you wanna do the pull-
ing?   How do you do it? Do you put
                                       it between your legs?
Yeah.   Do you just pull?
Yeah.   Oo, oo.
What?   Nothing.
Stand up. You get more lever-
age.   No, no, it's better this way. I
                                       can't do it if I stand up. I'm a
                                       woman.
What have you got against
standing up?   I'm a woman.

                    Sound of cork popping.

                                       There, I didn't spill it either.

Oh god, I've got to cut the
roast beef. Why didn't you tell
me?   Well, because there it was . . .
The table's all cluttered up.
Get some of this stuff off the
table . . .   I can't. We'll need everything.
Well but it'll scatter all over
and it'll break.   Here. Move it over here and get
                                       everything far away. You have
                                       a lot of control with that knife
                                       it won't scatter.

Let's see if this wine is really
good.

I thought they were pieces of
bread.

I don't know what you're talking about.

Who said that?

Do I think you could have it?
Yeah, you could have it.
Why couldn't you have it? It
wouldn't be much fun.

I wonder if the microphone is
picking everything up. Maybe
it's not loud enough.
Maybe it's not loud enough.
Maybe I should put it louder.

I feel very cranky.

I dunno.

Say it's gonna spill all over, get
that out of the way.

I like to eat potatoes like pieces
of bread. See?

Uh. They look like garlic bread.
Tad's Steak House.

Do you think you could have a
fake roast beef meal in which
you invite people over for roast
beef and serve them everything
else including the gravy?

And then, you just never come
out with the roast beef and
everybody's too embarrassed to
mention it.
I said do you think you could
have that?

It would be a happening. When
everybody leaves then you can
eat all the roast beef yourself.

Hmm?

Maybe.

Good night for a recording.
How come?
Well, once you get the roast
beef cut you won't have anything else . . .

Look that's partly cut, that's

Well . . . what do you suggest?

Just make sure you get it in there. Or else start with the next piece.

I can't start with the next piece. It's an impossibility.

Then you cut this one off with another knife.

Girls' voices from outside: Lydia. Get in there. Get in. Hey you wanna get an ice-cream cone? Hey doggie. Get IN.

We should have some kind of platter to do this kind of cutting on.

We don't have one.

I know. I said we should have one.

Sounds of cutting and crockery.

It certainly is a huge roast beef.

Pawpy. Come on. Pawp. Come on. Pawpy. GET IN. GETINTHEHOUSE.

Well there's gonna be two thin slices and one thick one. Which do you prefer?

Two thin. We should share the end though.

Huh? I don't care about the end.

Oh I do.

All right take it. Here. It's about all I can stand to cut of the meat.

I'm the guy who said roast beef. I'd like to see a film by Peter Heliczer.

Well, is there one playing around?

Well they come and go, but. There isn't one at the moment I don't think.

Why would you like to see a film by Peter Heliczer?

I'm curious because he seems from what I know of him to be

more serious, or with a better backlog of real poetry than with most of the people working in film.

Well movies aren't poetry they're not interested in poetry.

No but there's a shallowness about them, that, uh, comes through. That makes you feel that they're gonna exhaust themselves. And because he's written real poetry that's why he might have more depth and more things to say. Thank you, that's really enough.

You want some of this juice? This wine is not good.

I think so.
Really? How does it compare to last night?

It's not that much better.

I wonder if the one that's a little more than this one is any good?

Well if you get a good year all the prices are supposed to be better.

What do you mean, they're all supposed to be good?

They're all supposed to be better. Than a bad year or a mediocre year.

Yeah but they should also be better than each other if they cost that much more.

Yeah, but then you shouldn't have to get such an expensive wine to get something decent.

But even this is very cheap for Beaujolais.

It is not.

Beaujolais is usually two dollars, isn't it?

It is not. It's one of the cheaper wines.
Do you put that on the meat or on the vegetable?

I don't know.

The potatoes are really good
with pepper.

Did you put salt and pepper on
mine?

No.

Sounds of eating.

Why don't we get the sharp
meat knives?

We don't use them.

I seem to have the only correct
interpretation to a lot of those
poems.

Of a lot?

Mm. And everybody else seems
to disagree with me all taking
one kind of one interpretation.

You mean in several poems
they do that? They all agree?

Yeah.

How does that make you feel?

That either I or they are stupid.
Well, I think I'm right, but it
makes me feel a little uh,
slightly shaky. You know I
have to I keep going back over
them and I keep coming back
to the conclusion that I'm
right.

I know. Which which one?

Mmhm.

I'd have to call it a waste of
time.

Do you have to read them?

Yeah.
And also I wonder how much
should I be polemical. And
how much should I let it stand
as self-evident.

Well apparently you don't have
room to be polemical.

The end piece tastes like dog
hairs.

Wonderful. Don't eat it.

I don't know sometimes things
taste that way to me when
they're not that way.

Do you think it's not that good?

Not fatty *enough?* Think so?
Could've been a little more
rare.

Better to overestimate. No.
Better to make it rarer, than
well done.
Then you can always. . . . Oh
you mean then you put it back
in again?

Oh I see. Oh.
Hard to cook in this oven.
Hard to cook in this oven.

It's good.
It's not fatty enough.
Didn't make enough gravy.

I know. Wasn't my fault. Flame
in oven goes up high even when
you set it low.

I already did.

No. I made it what I thought
would turn out to be rare. And
when I first looked it wasn't
any more.

Hmm?

Eating sounds.

Good though.

Okay. What?
What?
Pretty stupid.

Somebody made an acute observation in the paper. That
dope Andrew Sarris.
You know what it was?

I think he must suffer from
having to write that thing every
week. On all those stupid
movies oh well. He said that
that all the tired movie vamps
seem to come from Scandina-
via.

Want to say something stupid?
Dombeydupois.
Dombeydupois.
I can't think of anything stu-
pider.

Mmhm.
No, but he's acute sometimes.
What'd he say?

But he must like writing it.

Sweden.
Torrid.

And I think that's true. He puts it as a question. I agree with him. Did you?

No. Although that's the myth.

Right. But Sophia Loren wasn't, isn't. Wasn't. And she still seems frigid.
Separated from her sex.

Mm.

Mm.

Intermediate?   Whatdyamean intermediate?

Like you?

All the tired ones?
Torrid. Oh right. And the Italians are very cold.

Mm-hm. But that isn't very hard to figure out. First of all no one says if you come from a hot country you have to be hot. Second of all. They come from a Catholic country where they're very separated from their sex.

Wasn't what?
Well, she's a Catholic. I mean she comes from a Catholic country. Where the image of women is a certain thing. I can't imagine an Italian woman of an intermediate kind.

A kind of, a kind of sexy companion type.
Yeah, like me.

Sound of truck going by.

I'm changing my mind about the wine. As I drink it.
As I drink it.

Mm? Better?

I made a crater around my potato. Now it's my pocrater.

You know what things are in here? I wanna compare it with the other one. Tomatoes celery carrots beets parsley spinach

What's in the other one?
Could you repeat that again
more slowly?

sweet green peppers lemon
juice citric acid and salt.
I don't know.

An exhilarating blend of the
extracted juices of fresh tomatoes, celery, carrots, beets,
parsley, spinach, and sweet
green peppers, to which salt,
concentrated lemon juice, and
citric acid have been added.

Which do you like better do
you say?
I think the other probably has
more vegetables.

The other.

The other one? Oh that's good.
Yeah. Especially if they lie
around in tin cans for a while
after they're open—that really
increases it.

It has more taste. It tastes more
like tin cans.
I like that taste.

Does?
Why?

Why?

You know something about being on tape makes you very
sarcastic.
Yeah, you must feel repressed.
It must make you self-conscious.
Because I think sarcasm is self-
conscious style.

Oh you mean it makes *me*
sarcastic.
Oh I'll bet you're right.
What am I gonna do about
that? Dya think it makes you
sarcastic?

Yeah.

Also I'm aggravated, that's another thing that's making me
sarcastic.

No I think it makes me something, I don't think I can tell
what it is.

About what?

About the critics.

I have to read them and rethink everything and decide I'm
right. And very rarely do I decide I'm wrong.

Well, I have to read them.
Mm?
No. I don't know.

Sounds like it. I guess I won't
use it any more.

What is the name of this kind
of roast?
No, really.
Really? This is the best kind
then.
Where'd you get it?
You want my opinion of it?
I like it but I don't think it's
that good. That good quality
as it should be. Do you?
They do?

No, I don't think so mm-mm.
It may be . . .
I don't know. It may be that
Key doesn't have the best kind
of meat in the really expensive
meats.

I don't think they'd have par-
ticularly good roast beef but
they'd have cheap roast beef
probably.

Oh. About them being wrong?
Or about your having to read
them.

Mm-hm. Maybe you shouldn't
bother to read them.
Is rethink a real word?
Is rethink a real word?
Or is it a Kennedy Administra-
tion word?

You can have more peas if you
want them.

ROAST BEEF.
Really. Silver tip.

Mm-hm.
Key Food.
I don't like it.

They vary all the time.
Mm-hm. Maybe it's just too
well done.
Isn't there another kind that's
really great?

Or maybe certain people want
me to go to the A&P. And walk
the depressing aisles.

This is cheap it's (laughing)

Is that cheap?

only a dollar fortynine a pound. I think it's expensive. It's not cheap.

How about a short story called Prices?
Prices.

Crisis?
Prices. Oh. Okay. Okay. A dollar ninetyeight.
Oh. When?

Not to be done now.
I don't know. My brother's sociology course is being taught by someone who doesn't like sociology but likes literature.

That's nice. Is it a sociologist?

Mm-hm. So, my brother, said, he told them they were going to read novels. And, I asked my brother what novels they were going to read so the first novel they're going to read is Truman Capote's new novel—which isn't a novel. But that's all right they're reading Camus too.

How's he working it into sociology. Maybe he's using Coser's book and approach.

Yeah probably. And he's probably, he'll just point out elements of sociology. Maybe he can point out um, through disintegration what what things exist.

Through disintegration?

Yeah like, the family is disintegrating, so I suppose modern fiction would show how the family is disintegrating. Like mother died yesterday or something. So then you learn about the family through disintegration.

Sounds good.
Yeah. You don't need a novel

Are you kidding?

to tell you that. All you need is
a sentence would do.

What's the teacher called?

What's the teacher called?
This wine makes me very hun-
gry.
Do you want some?
It's really good wine.
It's a vintage year, a great year.

Mm.

A crop, yeah.

We should have the sharp steel
knives because we're cutting
meat. Right?

Well I just made that up. It's
my idea you know it's not his.
And if you don't like it you can
stuff it down your brain.
He's called Max. I don't know.

Good.
No.

Is that what a vintage year
means.
But what's a vintage? Literally.
Isn't that just a year?
A crop from the vines, right?

Yeah.
How about gentian violet for
dessert?

Liquid pouring.

What is this tiny onion?

You want some more peas?
Huh?
Gee they have a lot of onions
in here.

No.

Give me one, okay?
Thank you. You brought a pea
with it.

Do you think this conversation
is going to prove interesting?
To outsiders?

No.
I find it dull at the moment myself. I suggest that we erase it.

Maybe you'll change your mind
when you hear it.

Maybe.

This story is called Plaster Cast.
Like Segal.

Why?
Oh.

ROAST BEEF 115

It's also called Candid Snap
no Candid no Candid no . . .
Snapshot it's called Snapshot.

I thought it was called Roast
Beef.

It's called Roast Beef too.
It's also called, concrete literature.

It's also called, The Vast Drag.

Eating sounds.

I wonder if the microphone can
hear our eating sounds.
You think it can?

I think it can.
I think of it as a live ear. Very
impartial. Very cold. Nasty in
fact.

You're much closer to it than I
am, maybe it can only pick up
your sounds.

What would you think of that?
That would be annoying,
wouldn't it?

Mm. Do you feel it's inter-
fering?
Our life?

With what?
(Sigh.) No, not really.

Dog barking outside.

I don't think I'd be saying much
anyway.

Maybe you'd be saying a lot
more.

Dog barks louder and continually.

Woof-woof, woof-woof.
Mm? Really?
Well have some wine.
Well maybe we have one Vege-
mato.
Whose dog is that?
I think we should keep these

I drank a whole can already.
Yeah, and I want more.
No I really don't want wine.

No there isn't any more.
Mmnmm.

things in an album, and look at
them when we're old. If we're
old.
                                        That's too much like Beckett.
Did you read that?   I heard about it.
I heard about it too, I haven't
read it.
Man I'm still hungry, I'm
getting hungrier and hungrier.
What am I gonna do I think
I'll have some more meat.
Okay?   Mmhm.
Okay with you? Do you want
more?
Remember how cranky I was at
the beginning?   Yeah.
Now I'm not, now I'm getting
euphoric.   Good.
(Groan.)

Sounds of cutting.

It's not soft enough.

No it's not. It's not that good
meat. Maybe we should take
up Key Food in their guarantee
they give you.   What guarantee?
The guarantee that says you
can bring back the meat after
you've tried it.
                          Where does it say that you
                          mentioned that before and I've
I don't remember where.   never seen it.
                          You can't bring it back after
You can bring back the re-   you've eaten it.
mains.

                          That kind of thing appeals to
                          me less than anything else that
                          I can think of.
Well it's not that bad anyway.
It's good.   I hate doing things like that.

Me too. Everybody does.

Like who?

Anyone you know?

That's true.
(Falsetto): "Take your greasy
chicken back." Can you imagine slapping meat particles
down on the counter . . .

I'm still very hungry but what
can I do?
Would you like some more
peas?
Yes?

Whatdyamean what about en-
dearments?

Endear me.
Now you mean?
I could be endearing if I wanted
to.
What?
Dear Lynn. You are very en-
dearing. You are a dear.

Eating probably makes it
rough. If it bothers enough get
that stuff before the places
close.

Mm-mm. Some women like it.
I think some women thrive on
it.
Women who have nothing else
to do. Or argumentative
women.
No. I think your mother likes
to return things to department
stores but I don't think she likes
conflicts.

Slapping chicken soup on the
counter.

Eat the flowers.

Mmm.
No I wouldn't. What about en-
dearments though?

Are they allowed, suppose I
want to be endearing?
No, suppose you wanted to.
Yeah.

Let's hear it.
Let's hear it.

(Giggles.)

I think that sore bothers me
more now.

What's it called again, Crystal
Set?

Chrysomatic? Schenectady?

How do you think it would be
living in the Vermont woods
all winter?

In a frame house.

Yeah.
I don't mean warm, I mean
how would you like it?

I guess it would be good.
I guess it would be good.
Maybe I should call *****
up right after dinner. You
think it's too late?

No, but if I stay there for two
years you can.

Oh that's true.
Hm. Hm. That's true.

Oh boy, here I am in my replacement I mean my status as
a replacement again. Tempo-
rary. Academic Temporaries.

That's true.

Lipswitch?
Now I'm having some water.
Wouldn't it be nice if you
wanted to drink something you
could just open a hole in yourself and let the water in? Like
**** ****** used to do.

Ah, it depends on what shelter
we had.
You mean a frame house like
you find in Massachusetts?
Well, they keep warm.

Oh, I think it would be very
beautiful. For a single winter
I'm sure I'd like it.
We'd have to shovel the snow.

But Ronnie, I can't live in a
house in the Maine woods in
the winter, I have to be in New
York.

Well, did anyone say it's for
two years maybe someone is on
a sabbatical. How do you know
it's for two years.
Maybe some fellow has gone
crazy and he's just out for nine
months.

Well you're not sure.
And that's what you wanna be
anyway.
Also maybe then there'd be an

That's true too.

opening once you got there, you don't know that.
(Laugh.) You know those jokes where where they depend on the piling up of fantasy until the person forgets to refer to the original fact and then goes flying off, like I can hear you calling ***** and (laugh) and your saying (laugh) well what about the driveway (laugh), will I have to shovel the driveway (laugh).

I know what the trouble with this story is that you can't laugh.
Lynn.
I think you should get that other stuff because it's an anesthetic too, and it'll stop it from hurting. Wouldn't that be a big relief?

What?

Why? You haven't been out all day.
It'd be an anesthetic and it would cure it faster. Wouldn't you like that?
Chrysomint.

(Sigh.) I don't want to go downstairs.

I don't know.

Synechdoche.

Yeah, what's it called?
(Laugh.) Oh please don't make me laugh.
Metonymy.
Oxymoron. Plymo.

No it had something to do with cure, or sect. In-sect.
No-sect.
Chloro-sect. No. What is the word that has to do with bio . . .
Biotics.
No.

It's chloro.

Biotics.
It wasn't Chlorobiotic. Was it?
But it's something like that.

Mmm.

You better get this other stuff then. Was it tomorrow morning?
Uh, wash the dishes, that will get it off.
Seriously.
But it will.

No the dishes it's soaking that gets it done.

Well, it's the constant water and soap.
What?

All right.
Well what's the what's it called I think we're being very self-conscious.
You're putting it on.

All right. (Snap.) I just turned it off.

Chlorosept. Wasn't that it?
Chlorosept?
I'll call him up.

Ahh . . .

Look at this ridiculous nail.
What am I gonna do about that I have to go to *******'s office tomorrow morning. I can't be all purple for that.

Mm-mm.
They're yours.
Listen I know it won't because I rubbed Ajax into it.

I don't soak my hand when I do the dishes.

Okay I'll tell you what.
We are about to arrange a real balance of. . . . I'll wash all the lousy dishes, if you'll get me the thing.
Ah, once again the division of labor male and female the female . . .

I guess so well turn off the microphone.

Call your father again okay?
Chloromint. Chlorodene.

Chloroseptic. I don't know.
You can go to the drugstore and ask the druggist and then if he doesn't know you can call your father from the drugstore. You can also weigh yourself. And while you're down there could you weigh me? And could

Do we have any dessert?
I'm still hungry.
I don't want cheese.
Mm.

you weigh what's left of the roast beef?
No.
Cheese if you want.
Cheese if you want.
I wish Andy Warhol were making a movie of this instead of just a tape. Eating dinner he could call it Slob—which stands for Sukenicks love onions best. Right?

Mm. ********* saw that movie he made called Suck Off. He said it was very good.
Yeah.
Yeah. He said it made you concentrate on . . . hemidemisemiquavers of . . . changes of expression. It made you concentrate and really see the flicker of change, each flicker of change that flickered across the fucker's face.

How is it?
Are you kidding? Did he really?
He really liked it?

Yes.

Mm.
I guess you're not interested.

What do you see one man's face and nothing else?
You don't see his genitals or anything.
Too bad.
I'm hemidemisemiquaveringly interested.
His Fire Island movie was playing last week.

What's his Fire Island movie about?

Are you kidding?
Are you serious?

What kind of thing?

Why do you like that?

It's called My Hustler and it stars Johnny America.
No.
No, and I really like that kind of thing. I mean I . . .
That kind of Johnny America, I like that.
I don't know it appeals to me

although I don't think the movie would be very good. And I also like the title of Gerard Malanga's poems that he was reading.

What's that?

At a reading last week. They're called The Debbie High School Drop-out Poems.

Oh that's wonderful.
No.
No.
I don't know, it sounds like something on the back of a Co-ets box. What's a Co-et?

You don't like them?
Hm?
Why not?

A Co-et is something that doesn't sound like what it is. All it is is what you use to wipe off makeup with.

Oh.
Yeah.

But it sounds worse, doesn't it?

How are you feeling now?
Okay I'll get some of that stuff. But remember you got the peroxide. You wanna try some wine?

My mouth really bothers me.

I'd like to taste it anyway as a matter of fact.

It's good, it's fuller-bodied than last night. But it still has a little sharpness to it that I don't like.

Not sharpness, coarseness. And a sort of deadness. It's got nothing bubbly and light and happy about it. Like Beaujolais has. At its best.

Maybe the other year, fifty-nine or whatever it was that we used to get was better than this.

Maybe they rushed these—no. It's not bad though it's pretty good. I call it cistern wine.

Why?

It feels like it comes out of a
very still cistern.

Why do you say your sister
deserves special credit?

Because she was a big influence
on me at an important point
that helped me get out of find
my way out of Brooklyn.

Really, what were you at that
point?

Well, between sixteen and
twenty. Twenty-one.

Even after you were out of
school.

Yeah.

Did you get it off your teeth?
You still look sort of funny.

Well I stopped trying very hard
because I know I have to put
it on again.

I think it's a good idea to
get that stuff because at least
it avoids discoloration you
know?

Mm. It's so impractical, I don't
see how you can do it without
getting some discoloration. On
your tongue at least.

A lot of things happened today.
The fuck-up about the Press.
A lot of things to get you uh,
there's dessert. Those cookies.

What?
Mm-hm.
          ⊙
Oh. I'm sorry I forgot about
that.

A lot of things to make you
unstable and uh to make your
life undecided.
I don't mind that kind of thing
I rather like it.

Yeah.

Me, me. Right I was thinking
well this is change, we were
just talking about change, why
should you get upset about anything it's just change.

Right, it's change. But it's
change for the worse.
Right, not necessarily.
Would you get me my toothpick please. The one with the
ivory and gold uh trimmings.

Yes. And the onyx shoe horn.

Yeah I wanna put my shoes on
my teeth.

Are they ready?

Yeah, I guess so.

Hey this is pretty spooky.
Little guy between first and
second tavern.
First and second tavern.

And it's a dark night lit only
by a lantern . . . or a lan-
thorn.

Why is it funny?

Yeah it is strange. Maybe he
wouldn't maybe he'd wander
over the countryside.

Not necessarily.

And the trellis work on the
bottom?
Why, do you wanna put on
your shoes?

Oh listen maybe you can get
the Woodstock pictures too.
I'll give you the little ticket.
He said this week, which is
very specific of him but but
it's the end of this week.
Are you finished?

What is it?

Between what?
Is that the place it's only three
miles to go. Are you sure they
have Pepperidge Farm cookies?
Yes.

I think the funny thing is that
he has no choice, whether they
have the cookies or not.
I mean it's silly. He'd go there
anyway what does he care?

Sounds of dishwashing.

I think it's the famous lemon
cookie murder.

Mm.

By the kids in lemon colored gloves, remember that poem? The kids in the lemon colored gloves? The Patchen poem?

By the what?

Wait a minute, that sounds familiar. It's a Patchen poem.
Hum-mm-um.
Vaguely.
Vaguely.

The poem goes Wait, wait, wait, wait, wait, wait, wait, wait, now.

Sounds of dishwashing.

Dialogue, you know, between two people, should be written on either half of the page, as opposed to one thing after the other.

U-u-h, that was that trick in *****'s book.

Oh that's true, that was a telephone conversation.

I think it's rather obvious in concept.

I think it's obvious as a trick, but I think as a real, as a convention, it makes sense.

You mean going all the way through. Maybe. You got a point there, maybe I should type this up on two different sides of the page.

The way we talk anyway because we're always interrupting each other.

Right, yeah. Especially you me. Right?
Mm-hm-hm-hum-hmn-hm.
Can I have coffee before I go out to get your stuff?
Yes I really do. I really really really do. I can't tell you how much I do. Do do do. Do. Hey

The other way around.

You really want it? Should I make it?

how about a little sex in this
story?
I mean a little sex. You wanna   Whaddyamean?
put a little sex in this story?   Okay.
Huh.   Okay.
Okay.   How do we do it?
You have to come close first.   Huh?
You have to come close first.   Okay. What about the coffee?
What about the what—yes the
coffee, yeah.   How can I come close and
                                         make the coffee?

You can, I'll if you stand in
front of the stove I can pinch
your ass. Then you can go,   Okay. That sounds nice and
Oo-oo   oo-oo-oo,   and   I'll   premeditated.
say, Garlic squeezer, garlic
squeezer.
It is premeditated. All right I
won't do it I won't do it. But
I really do, wanna have coffee.
I feel very intense about that.   I'm making it now. I'm making
                                         you coffee.

                    Sounds of water, dishwashing.

(Sings): When April showers,
may come your way, they bring
the flowers . . . that reminds
me of Bowers, which reminds
me of the course, which bloom
in May . . .   Could you make the coffee?
Yes I could. Could you give me
a spoon, oh you gave me one.   Hm?
Nothing. How   many   more
meals do we get out of this do
you think?   I don't know.
Mmmm-hm.

Could you light it?   Yeah. Was that someone who
                                         predicted cannibalism?

Yes.
A demographer.

I didn't.

Oh, good point. Except it's not
being acted out.

Mm. That's true.

Well it's very perverse in a way
because it makes you very conscious. Right?
It makes you know you're alive
really, that's it. In a way in
which you don't wanna know
it. Or in any case, shouldn't
care about it.
What?

Yeah, I'll do it. But uh, he
probably won't have any answer. Well you gotta try a little
peroxide too, why don't you
try washing it with peroxide.
That will do the trick.

Who?

Ronnie, you lit the stove.
Oh. With one hand, from a
distance of ten feet. With the
match in his mouth.

You know what this is like, this
is like a play in reverse, plays
are written so they can be
acted out—this is acted out so
it can be written.

Yes it is. Because aren't you
sitting here while I'm washing
the dishes, but that wouldn't
go into any page page render-
ing of this, and I thought:
sounds of dishes being washed.
And then I thought, that's a
stage direction.

Yeah.

Nothing.
You might also ask the man
how I get gentian violet off
my lips.

I never had one of these before.

One of which?
Hey do you have a knife? I mean could you hand me a knife?
A sharp thin steel one. Or a fat chrome one, I don't care. Any one. And could you get me the crackers from up there? Huh? Thank you.

I have to say that I found the young man before the mirror very repulsive.
In a fleshly way.
I just thought flesh flesh flesh its dripping off him. He's too fleshy.
Didn't you find him physically repulsive in some way?
No?
I've known kids who are physically repulsive in that way.

Yeah. They're usually All-American-Boy types. Or some funny variation on that.

I imagine Jack Armstrong as that type. Why do you think Otto is jealous of people with muscles?

Well . . .

A sore like this.

What kind?

The what? Oh.
Why?

I just found him comic.

No.

Nor was he meant to be. You mean physically in good shape but repulsive?

I think Otto is jealous of people with muscles.

Because for some reason when I walked into Anna's house he started this conversation about Hannah. About whom I have no interest whatever, and I can't really conduct a conversation with him about Hannah because I didn't know her. And of course Anna didn't know

How . . .
Has he seen her recently?

Jealous? Of her husband?

What'd he protest about?

I thought he liked him.

Oh I'll never be able to publish this.
I'll never be able to publish
this.
There are too many unspeakable things in it.
Although Otto is pretty muscular, isn't he?
Yeah he's little but he's
strong.

You want coffee yet?
Why, because you didn't have
any wine, huh?
Could you let me have the
strainer?
The strainer let me have the
strainer?

who Hannah was. And we were
talking about her husband.
No, she just disappeared. And
he was talking about her husband, and it seems, I thought
he was really jealous.
Of his muscles. I mean he
really protested too much like,
if I talked about a girl that
way everybody would jump on
me like mad, and tell me how
jealous I was.
Oh he just thought he was so
. . . pseudovirile and so
on . . .
All the more reason he should
be jealous.
Whereas men get as jealous as
women only women are much
more honest about it.

Huh?

Why?

Oh.

He's very little Ronnie.

Well that's not what I mean,
people who have obviously
good physiques.
Yeah. Now I'm in a bad mood.

No, because of my lip I guess.

What?

Yes, I will.
What, yes. Can I have the strainer?

Well we'll let it warm up before we drink it.
No. Why should it be bad?

Well, if we don't chill it it'll . . .

If we don't chill it it'll spoil.

I gave you a little less.

A few things I think.
Personal things. I mean that mentioned names.

I'll tell you what, we could say we we can say anything like that you know and then let's take it out, what the hell.
Right?
Like in the Ithaca story, right?
Right?
Right.

Whaddyamean.

Oh, would you put the cork back on?
Do we have to chill it now?
You sure? You sure?
But if red wine is chilled it isn't good.

Isn't that bad?
I don't know. I would think changes of temperature would affect the wine badly.

It might have sensitive molecules.
I should have water when I have wine because I drink wine when I'm thirsty.

That's all right.

Have you wanted to say anything that you've repressed?
Me too.
Yeah.
Oh. That's true, I shouldn't I shouldn't have done that.

Right.

Right.
But there are certain things that it seems to me are beyond the decorum of a situation aside from personal names.
I don't know, certain remarks . . . just wouldn't go down right.

Such as? Tell me one.
Ah, tell me one.
Ah, please, gee.

I don't know.
No. I can't think of any now.
Mm. Mmm.
Wanna play Nick and Nora
Charles? O-o-h Ni-ick (giggle).
Oh Nick, (laugh), Nick (giggle).

You mean sexy things is that
what you mean? We can always
cut them . . .
Such as.

No, no. Not sexy, indecorous.
Don't ask me because I'm not
supposed to say bad words.
Say bad words.
God said.
(Sneeze!) What?
No.

You're not supposed to *what*?
Who said?
Ah come on no kidding.
Do you smell paint?

Aren't you gonna save the
juice?

Uh, should I save it in here?
Do you think? Do you think
it will work if I put it in
there?

Won't it drip out you better
put it in there. Or maybe it's
not worth saving, I don't know.

No it is worth saving it's very
precious, cause this gets very
dry. I'll put it in a cup.
Oh my god I really feel like
a monster today.
I really feel like I'm dragging
my body around.

Why?

U-u-u-h, you don't look like
a monster. Mmm, you look nice
and sweet. You look like
feathers. You look like chocolate cookies. You look like
hot rolls. You look like furry.
(Kiss sound.) Infectious mono-
nucleosis.

Isn't it only infectious if you
put your tongue inside your
mouth?

Love o love o foolish l-o-ove,
Love o love o foolish l-o-ove,
Love o love o foolish love,
Love o love o foolish hands.
What's that called again, Tri-
cerotops?
Chlorotops? Chloro*sox*?

It's called Chloro something.
Also get instructions because
maybe your father has the all-
fire way of curing yourself
within three hours by making a
hole in your mouth.

Well I'm sure it will give instructions on the bottle. Aren't
you? What?

I guess so.

Those are comic book club
cookies.

All you have to do is be careful to enunciate clearly.
Like non dip-thong club. Now
you give me the lecture on
dip-thong. Followed by the
lecture on ah ampi-theater.
Ampi-the-ater.

When?

I only give those lectures once
a year.
I have to get up very early in
the morning.

What time?
Why?

Eight.
Cause I have to be there at
ten.

At ten? Then you can get up
at nine, you can make it by
ten.

How can I, I'd have to leave
at a quarter after nine to get
there by ten I can't get out
that fast.

No you get there in a half an
hour.

Not quite a half an hour. I
think.

You better hurry up.
Us. To finish dinner.
The tape must be almost fin-
ished.

Who?

Is it really? It may just last.
I'll bite into a cookie. And
crunch munch. What's in these,
oh, they're crunch cookies, hah
hah.

Munching sounds.

This is very funny.

Which is very funny? I already observed that.

I know but, coming to it myself
seems to make it funny.

Munching sounds.

Guess what kind of nuts is in
here?

Peanuts?
Pecans?
Pembrokes?
Filberts?
You misled me. Philoden-
drons?
I give up.

Mm-mm.
Mm-mm.
You mean filberts.
No.

No.
It was the kind that was found
in there was found in Familia.

Elms?
(Laugh.) What kind?
No, really, what kind?
Oh.
Remember how we used to get
hazel nuts in Spain? And how
bad they tasted?
I don't know. At the *Marché*.

(Munch munch munch.)
Cedar nuts.
Hazel nuts.

Sometimes . . .

No. Where'd we get them?
(Laugh.) If you don't stop
making me silly I'm gonna
throw the potatoes toward you.

Do you like these cookies?

Mm not bad. Do you have a
sore throat?   No I have a sore lip.
                                        Which of the drugstore guys
                                        told you to get this.
The old nutty benevolent one.   Oh. He's not benevolent.
No?   I don't think so.
(Yawn.)   I don't think he'd really help
                                        anyone, unless he'd really see
                                        something in it for himself.

He'd say, I've been in this
neighborhood for thirty years
as a druggist and I've never
helped anyone, unless I saw
something in it for myself.
Because it's not worth it other-   The tailor . . .
wise, he'd say. Otherwise it's
not worth it.   said to me as a joke, the day
                                        I brought my coat in, I've only
                                        been a tailor two and a half
                                        years.
Really?   It wasn't a joke. I mean it was
Maybe it wasn't.   a joke, but that's what he sews
                                        like.

Maybe it wasn't.
Isn't he running that store
now?   I wish his son were running it.
Mm.   His son was really good.

Whaddya suppose his son is
doing, starting another store?   Yeah, probably.

I think I have the sore throat
from that smell. I think it's
coming up through the floor.
What do you think?   One of my favorite words is
                                        depuis.

Mm, very nice. What about
what I just said?   I don't want to talk about it.
The purple's coming off.   Where?

Your finger.

Yeah.

Lemme see your mouth.
It's going off a little. Oh it's
still on your tongue.

Me, I wouldn't put that stuff in
my mouth.

I don't remember. I'm sure I've
had it.
There it go-o-oes. It's over.

Is there less than there was
before?
Is it coming off my mouth?
Should I wash the dishes with
my mouth?

Didn't we once put it in your
mouth?

No, really, no kidding, I seem
to remember your tongue being
purple once like that.

WHAT'S YOUR STORY

The moon is out and full. The sky is that near blue of bright clear
nights, so bright that one can see only a few of the brightest stars.
On the horizon the sharp, barren mountains, then the desert, like
a sea. Here the barren ground, the vulnerable figure protected by
its sleep, and that peculiarly self-contained lion. One assumes
he—or is it she—is asleep, though from the look of the face he
might be dead, the skin blackened by the desert sun. This perhaps
would explain the quiescence of the lion. Natural repugnance for
dead meat strike carrion. Leather bones rotten meat. Dead one
would say, from the odd angle of the feet protruding from the
robe strike striped robe that could be by Noland or Morris Louis,
from the exposed teeth, the eyes open perhaps very slightly. Or
is he about to awake, the eyes opening strike the eyes on the
point of opening, to confront the lion with his stick and his
mandolin, or is it lute, by his side. Next to the lute, we'll call
it a lute, a brown jug, of water let's hope, then a thick band of
white, then brown, white, brownish-white, muddied water, snow,
rotting ice, a boat making its way through ice floes, a person in
the bow pushes aside a floating cake of ice with a stick and his
foot, others pole the boat, in the stern one man handles the
rudder, in the center a man standing one foot on the gunwale,
hand on knee, cocked hat, sword, big nose, behind him a flag,
American, partly furled. One would say it's cold out there. This
scene repeated again again again, a fleet of facsimiles, it heads
for a slightly projecting, off-white vertical, a recess, another nar-
rower vertical of the same color, snow on the ground, part of a
stone wall—large rocks trimmed with snow—a tree trunk rising
from the ground straight, a brown tangle of bushes, a snowy field,
at the left a road recedes, curves, and disappears further to the

left, cutting through bare trees, brown bushes, green pines, misty
distance, background of grey sky through bare boughs strike
background of grey sky through lattice of bare boughs. High, a
jet growls once, twice, fades. Drip of melting snow from eaves. A
gunshot echoes through the distance. I look to the left through a
window at right angles to the first: black boughs, a road, snowy
field, low wall of piled rocks, woods, horizon of soft contoured
hills, grey light of wintry afternoon. The bright morning light
floods the fields, lights up the woods, shapes the hills. The field
beyond the road is brown and green with patches of snow. The
air is blue, the breeze a blue breath, the trees sway at the bottom
of a sea of blue. Heavy grey clouds lower over the brown, barren
flatland. Pit in concentric pit lay sunken in the center of a huge
concavity, mud-yellow, rimmed by a rutted road. Greasy black
smoke against dirty grey sky. Gulls like swarms of flies hover,
drift, swoop in a huge, slow vortex, screaming like Harpies. A
shaft of late afternoon sun strike a shaft of yellowish late afternoon sun glints off broken bits of tin, shattered glass, then disappears. The fires redden the deepening shadows. One cannot see
much in the cobbled court, the limestone blocks of the building,
windows like a Renaissance palazzo. The smoky, lucent, humid
winter air, pearl-grey, seeps down to the bottom of the court.
From where I sit at my escritoire, and from there only, I can see
out the courtyard through an arch, through an arch through
an arch through an arch, beyond a slim, distant, tapered column,
a dark massive monumental arch suspended in the haze. There
is so much movement down in the street it is as if one were
watching strike as if one were looking into a motley collection of
fish in an overcrowded tank, frightened by an occult cause, rather
than at men women children dogs cats babycarriages carts cars
trucks buses. The noise is so constant it is part of the landscape,
like the tenements across the avenue. Here there is no weather.
Large flakes of soot fall visibly from the sky. The atmosphere
consists of carbon, sulphur, oxides that displace the air and seep
through the windows. From the courtyard unbelievably loud a
brokenhearted lover wails a high fidelity lament in an incomprehensible dialect of Spanish. The hills are absent beyond the visible
circumference of misty woods within which the fields, green-
brown, patches strike occasional remnants of last night's flurries,
the road to where it curves. The mist glows with its own inner

light, very *intime,* tracing the nearer trees in heavy chiaroscuro, the more distant trees rise like ghosts from a graveyard. The woods lack depth. Light filters between the trunks from somewhere offstage. A clump of pines looms heavy, without color. Mist muffles bare boughs, hangs from the tips of branches in shimmering drops. The stillness is part of the landscape, like the stone wall at the far end of the field that is there, but invisible. Now and then the house creaks the obscure complaints of its two hundred years. George Washington crosses the Delaware on the walls. Under the moon the lion watches, the figure sleeps, or wakes up, or rots. I sit at my desk and gaze into the mysterious woods. The desk, square, classical proportions. One thinks of the richer Colonial houses, or better, English of the Augustan period. Its lamp, wood, glass, suggesting wick and whale oil, its shaded bulb an incongruity. We're getting to know one another, this desk and I, we're learning to get along. Already we're getting to be friends. There's a flat, clear, open quality about it, a lucidity, a balance, an obvious and unquestionable respectability. No there's nothing suspect about this desk, nothing secret or ambiguous, nothing baroque, nothing intense, nothing intricate. Nothing like desks where I've holed up and held out. Safe at last. The fields are bright, the desk is lit by a shaft of light coming through the woods, George Washington crosses the Delaware on the walls. Wild grey clouds scud low beneath the black sky, gulls flock and hover about this point or that, so many they seem more like swarms of flies. Fires flare along the sides of the pit, sending up thick black smoke that disappears into the black of the sky. The desk is a large black rectangle with drawers running down one side. The glossy desk-top reflects the light of the gooseneck lamp in one corner. In the center of the large black rectangle, the smaller white strike the white rectangle of an open notebook. The open page said: ever clearly known it and tested it. It was as though unperceiving I had awakened from the American dream of tomorrow to the flat truth of today. Black ink, my handwriting.

Why don't you get rid of that desk asked Joan. Relevant to nothing, as usual. Her large, dark eyes, with their distended irises, shone with the black luster of my desk-top as she stared at me with her characteristic vacant expression.

Why? I asked.

I don't know.

Look I have to work now. I had stolen the desk and I was fond of it.

I suppose you want me to leave she said.

What would you like to do.

She shrugged and started putting her clothes back on. She was a terrific piece of ass, a slim fertility goddess, dazed with too much fucking and too many abortions. Later, after I put her into a story, after a lot of aimless traveling, a sexual tourist, she wound up marrying an Iraqi sheik, and went to live in a harem in Baghdad. She was a passive lay but she liked it, and she never complained about anything. I felt a little bad about letting her leave like that, right after making love, but I knew she was sleeping with two other guys, both older and with a lot more bread than me, a student, and both of whom wanted to marry her. So what the hell. You wouldn't have thought so, but I loved Joan, with the kind of desperation you have when you love something that you want to get away from. I kept comparing her to Josephine, who I knew from around McDougal Street, another extreme case, but a kind I had a lot more respect for. Joan liked money, she liked glamor, she liked secrets, she liked to make her hole the subject of exciting high intrigue. Josephine didn't give a damn. She fucked who she wanted, when she wanted, how she wanted, and she didn't bother to make a secret of it. She never knew where her next penny was coming from. If she really liked a man she had his baby. She had two already and she took them wherever she went. She tossed over all the moral garbage we use for ballast, and she acted as if nothing could hurt her. Dead now. These were the crazy people I knew then, all extreme cases, all failures every one of them, driven way out by the grey fifties. I liked failures. I aimed at being one myself some day. I was living in Cambridge, a graduate student, surrounded by Harvard, Radcliffe, M.I.T. I lived across from the dump. It was more picturesque, in its way, than Harvard Square. I had one old friend there, a painter, even poorer than myself. I had traveled across country with him in an old Ford before we'd gone to college, Route 66, El Paso, Old Glory, Arizona to the Coast. You could see him getting crazier every day, psychoanalysis didn't help. He'd quit a high-paying job as a commercial artist, and did nothing but lay around his cheap apartment drinking and watching television. He never went out. Finally one day in a drunken stupor, he jumped out a third story window, landed on his head, got up, and took a cab to the hospital. If they'd had taller buildings in Boston he would have been killed. After that he pulled out of it, went to New York and eventually became a famous painter. Even now he walks around with a bent neck from that business. No one got out of that time unscathed. There wasn't much to that Cambridge apartment besides the desk and bed. Very ascetic. Between that and the dump across the street, which smelled to high heaven all the time of putrefaction or the rotten-egg smell of burning garbage—the real smell of Cambridge I always used to think—I wasn't set up to entertain. But it was there that I began to get visits from certain peculiar individuals, odd characters, who came without invitation and left, sometimes, before I would have liked them to leave. There was April Foxbite, who I knew from the Coast, for example, glowing, California vulgarian. There was Jack Gold, consummate square. I knew him through Josephine of all people, what did she see in him—the same thing I did? He had an old, oak, traditional, compartmented, pigeon-holed, rolltop desk, that at one time I thought I wanted more than any kind of desk that had ever stood on the face of the earth. One day I noticed a shiny black Cadillac pulling up outside. That in itself was a major event across from the dump. There was a knock on the door. It was Ruby Geranium.

Eh goombah.

A short thick figure, white fedora, dark glasses, heavy padded black cashmere overcoat, black double-breasted suit, white-on-white shirt, white silk tie with a portrait of an old woman in a black shawl painted on it.

You here? I said.

Just in from the Coast. A little business in the North End.

His knuckles were loaded with gold and silver, barbaric gems. He looked around, nodding, sneering.

So this is where you hole up. Who you hiding from?

I'm glad you like it.

You're not smart Ronnie. Looka this crap. He slapped his knuckles against a bridge table I used to eat on. It collapsed. Look at this look at this. He punched two left jabs at the plaster-board wall. He left two hollow, cracked depressions.

Where'd you get this desk he said. He tipped it up with two

fingers under a corner as if to see what it was made of. My notebook and pen went sliding onto the floor. Gee sorry he said. He
let it drop with a bang.

I stole it I told him.

You don't say. You stole it. That's not nice Ronnie. You
shouldn't do things like that. That's small time. You don't take
risks for peanuts. That's bush-league stuff. You're not smart. But
you got the right instincts. Whata you get outa living on peanuts
Ronnie? Come on, why you holed up? Who ya hiding from? He
put his foot on my notebook strike he stepped on my notebook
and pulled it toward him across the floor.

Take it easy with that I said.

Relax. I'm just tryin to set you straight Ronnie. Between pals,
you know what I mean. "It was as though," he read slowly, "un-"
what? What's that mean? What is this crap?

It's a story.

A story he exclaimed. What about, Mother Goose? You make
me mad Ronnie. He took a step toward me. He clenched his fist
to show me his rings. Don't waste my time. I come with a deal
for you between pals and you tell me you're writing Mother
Goose?

It's a story I said.

What story.

Suppose I put you in it. Then it would be about you.

Oh, about me. You're writing a story about me. That's nice.
Why didn't you say so? I like that.

Yeah, good.

I'll tell you what he said. How about puttin my tie in it? He
held out his tie. See that, that's a picture of my mother. Painted
right on. Put that in the story.

Well I don't know if there's room in this story I said.

Whatyamean no room.

I'll put it in another one I said.

Okay that's better. Say who's that dame you got comin in and
outa here all the time? The one who sometimes she comes at
night and leaves in the morning.

That's Joan, a girlfriend.

I mean is she a nice girl? You know what I mean?

Yeah she's a nice girl.

I mean do you make her you know what I mean fuck you you know what I mean? A nice girl like that?

Come on, it's none of your business.

Like I'm just tryin to set you straight Ronnie you know what I mean? Between pals. You shouldn't do a thing like that to a nice girl like that Ronnie. You want dames I can get you all the dames you want. But I mean a nice girl you know what I mean? That's what I call moral turpentine. What are you some kinda beatnik?

What's the deal Ruby?

The deal is I wanna cut you in. I wanna put you on the main line. I wanna get you outa hiding. It's simple. You don't know how to do things Ronnie. I just show you how to do things. Anything you want. You wanna write, radio, TV, ads, you wanna work in college even, whatever it is. Don't worry about it we got friends all over. You're smart Ronnie. You'll become a big man in no time. I'll show you how to do it, it's all the same. You don't even have to do anything for us. We wouldn't be so crude. We just want you to be a big man. We have only your interests at heart. We just want you to be a big success.

And then?

And then we just come and see you sometimes. That's all. Like old friends. We just come and see you sometimes. In case we need a favor. You know what I mean?

I'll think about it.

Yeah. Think about it. No rush. Do your thing. We'll be waiting. You'll come around. Because there's no place else. And when you come, you'll come all the way. You know what I mean? It's like in my line. You can't afford to be yellow. You're either on top or on bottom, that's the way it works. And pretty soon you get tired of the bottom. Just tryin to set ya straight Ronnie. Between friends. Wise up. Know what I mean?

A few days after Ruby Geranium's visit, there was another unexpected knock at the door.

Who is it?

Police.

Who?

Open up. Police.

I opened the door and found a tall bulky figure in a brown

fedora with the brim pulled down and an overcoat with the collar turned up so that I couldn't see his face.

All right Ronnie came a boozy baritone. Relax. Just routine. Sergeant GunCannon. Is that you?

Looks like we finally caught up with you, hey Ronnie? He pushed past me into the room.

I ignored his remark. GunCannon always talked like that. How long you been in from the Coast? I asked him.

I got a little business in the North End he said. All right Ronnie, why'd you do it?

Come on Sergeant, I didn't do anything.

Yes you have Ronnie. Everyone's done something. You're no different from anybody else.

Well is there anything special you had in mind Sergeant?

Just checking he said.

Same old Sergeant GunCannon I said. Put er there. He had both hands shoved deep into his overcoat pockets. He withdrew his right and thrust it at me. In it was a revolver, almost completely concealed by GunCannon's huge hand. That was the only thing that really scared me about Sergeant GunCannon. He had huge hands.

Ever seen this before Ronnie? He let the gun lie on its side in the palm of his hand. It had a pearl handle with a portrait of an old woman in a black shawl. It looked familiar, I didn't know why.

Never saw it before Sergeant. What's up?

He dropped the gun back into his pocket. Nothing he said. Just a few routine questions.

What's going on GunCannon? Are you still working in the movies? Is this a movie?

You've heard of Interpol? he said.

Yeah.

He nodded.

Why are you hiding out in this crummy place he asked me sharply.

I'm not hiding I said.

He looked at me with narrow eyes. Come on, this is a hideout, don't kid me. I know a hideout when I see one.

I live here because I have no money Sergeant.

That's a way of hiding Ronnie. You could make some money if you wanted. Who you hiding from?

I'm just trying to stay by myself and mind my own business.

You can't do that Ronnie. You got to pay your debt to society. Every man owes a debt to society.

Not me Sergeant. Not this society.

You're a loafer Ronnie. You're a parasite on the face of society. You got a debt to pay and one way or another you're gonna pay it. It's on the books. Why don't you go out and get a job. You might as well make a buck for yourself while you're at it. It's compensation. No one likes to work Ronnie. None of us likes what they make us do to earn a living. You think I enjoy going around making it hot for guys like you? I like you Ronnie. You're a nice fella. Only some of the things that you're into are pretty disgusting. You been keeping women here. You can't expect to get away with something like that.

No I haven't Sergeant.

Yes you have. You been keeping women here, you've been making them undress and lie down on your bed, and you've been fucking them. All night.

Prove it.

He shoved his hand deep into his pocket and pulled out an old dried-up used condom. Explain that he said.

It's not mine.

We got laboratory tests.

I deny it.

Then you been masturbating. You can't masturbate in Boston Ronnie. There's laws against it. That's a very serious offense. That's vice. We can always get you on a vice charge Ronnie. We can get anyone on a vice charge. Fucking and masturbating. I know people are corrupt Ronnie, but Jesus, you really beat the band.

Look Sergeant all I'm trying to do is get away from it all and be by myself. I don't like what I see so I try to get away from it. That's why I'm poor that's why I live here. Okay?

Yeah it certainly is a ratty setup, even for a graduate student. You know I been up to see the Dean, Ronnie. I took a look at your records. It seems like you don't even do your work very much. You're no graduate student you just wanna stay out of the

army don't kid me. What's your draft board again, forty? Where'd
you get that desk?

Somebody gave it to me.

You're guilty as hell Ronnie. On every count. I could book
you right now. You can't fool an old cop like me. Vice, draft
dodging, petty larceny, consorting with known criminals. Where's
Ruby Geranium?

Whatyamean?

Don't play dumb, where is he? Come on Ronnie I'm getting
tired of this. He took his huge hands out of his pockets and
started cracking his knuckles.

I never heard of the guy I said.

We know he came to see you. What did he want, where did
he go?

I never saw him I never heard of him.

He flexed his knuckles, opening and closing his huge hands,
then shoved them back into his pockets.

Okay Ronnie. We'll let it go for now. But I'll be seeing you.
I'll be seeing you. No matter where you are, Interpol will be
there too. And meantime let me give you a piece of advice between old friends. You got to make up your mind whose side
you're on. It don't matter which, but you got to pick a side.
Everybody got to play the game. Because if you don't, that's
when you get into trouble. Bad trouble. Understand?

The desk gleamed dully under its gooseneck lamp, with a sug-
gestion of depths, interiors, as one mused over it, elbows resting
on its glossy black. The small room, the cheap furniture, the
dump across the street, seemed muffled, muted, the desk absorbed
everything into its blackness till there was nothing left outside,
while within it gathered a potent concentration. The snow had
been falling still fell strike the snow had been falling still falls.
Outside, the fields, the road are a white blank, a mirror that
turns you back to yourself. The brown veneer of the square,
classical desk is so highly polished you can see your reflection
in it. I open my escritoire and sit down as one might sit down
at a harmonium. Under the lucent grey of the sky an invisible
rain darkens the grey of the limestone building, the grey of the
cobbled court. I look through the court, its arch, the arch, the
court, the arch, beyond which an opacity of mist. Toward the
gardens, the tapered needle, the boulevard, the monumental arch

I know are there, but invisible. Harmony, order. There I walked
each day through arches gardens courtyards to the Bibliothèque.
It was like living in an abstraction, a theorem, an equation in
which the unknown term was myself. Only I was haunted by
fellow expatriates, phantasmal tourists, Americans who wouldn't
leave me alone. Morris from the Bronx, bony sharp-faced green
complexion. He was here with Selma. His first trip to Europe, a
belated honeymoon, and the first and as far as I could see the
only thing that strikes him is the potential of the import-export
business. He always had a valise full of things like Swiss watches
German cameras Italian typewriters Spanish mantillas English
pipes Ukrainian babushkas Moroccan boxes Persian rugs Russian icons Greek antiquities Amsterdam diamonds French per-
fumes Havana cigars Chinese jade and spices from all the Asias.
He was always trying to sell me something. It didn't matter that
I had no money, or that I wouldn't buy anything if I had. He
knew that. It was just a tic. He related to the world in terms of
merchandise.

You got to buy a pair of these gloves Ronnie. You're crazy if
you don't. You can't get real French gloves at a price like this.
I'm selling below cost, a sacrifice. A bargain, a fire sale, everything must go. I'm selling out. Look at this watch, are you
kidding? At a price like that you should buy two of them. You're
crazy Ronnie, you have to buy something. You mean to tell me
you come to Europe, an American, and you don't even buy anything? With a discount for dollars? No import taxes? Come on
Ronnie, don't say no at least, say maybe. For Selma's sake. Let
me show you some of this German merchandise. I gotta sell you
something Ronnie.

Morris, you have to sell it but I don't have to buy it. Listen to
what I'm telling you. If you don't buy anything you don't have
to sell anything. That's one of the first things I figured out for
myself.

Look Ronnie, you see this scarf. Pure silk. I'm not going to
sell it to you. I'm gonna give it to you. Here, it's a present, take it.

I don't want it.

And all you have to do is buy this mantilla for your girlfriend.
The mantilla I'm giving you at a loss.

Then there was Walter, who was a real expatriate, that is, he'd
inherited money. There was something casual aimless disem-

bodied wraith-like about Walter. He was always urging me to stay in Europe.

What do you want to go back for? There's no place for you in the States. You know that.

There's no place for me here either Walter.

Of course not. You wanted to escape, and this is an escape. You have to face that. And once you make up your mind to escape, there's nothing to do but keep escaping. You have to keep moving, that's the answer.

What's the question?

Walter would always stir up the worst ghost of all, my doppel-gänger from the States, myself as graduate student, penance and purgatory, a purgatory which meant nothing, since I didn't be-lieve in paradise.

Eh goombah.

One day Ruby Geranium turned up at my door.

Just come up from Palermo he said. Thought I'd take a little vacation. He lumbered over to the escritoire and sat down in the red-plush chair that went with it, sweeping aside my papers. He looked around the room.

So, what are ya, on the lam, uh.

I'm not on the lam Ruby.

Don't tell me you're not on the lam. What else you doing in Paris. He glared at me, chin thrust out. Then he laughed. Come on let's be straight Ronnie, it saves time. I know you're on the lam. I'm on the lam too. Why don't we team up?

What are you talking about?

How you doing for cash Ronnie. You don't have to tell me, not so good. He thrust his hand into his pants pocket and grunting, pulled out a huge naked roll of bills. He licked his thumb, pulled off the top one, and without looking at it tossed it on the escritoire. It was a hundred dollars. Live it up he said. It's gonna be a long time before you have enough money to get to Paris again, a guy like you.

What's that for? I asked him.

Doncha wanna travel a little while you're in Europe Ronnie? He picked up my notebook by a corner, dangled it in front of my face for a minute, and let it drop on the floor. You don wanna waste all your time on this crap do ya? Live it up a little.

Take it easy with that I said.

Ever been to Italy Ronnie. Ah it's a beautiful country. I just
come back from there. You think Paris is good. I want you to get
a look at places like Roma, Napoli, Palermo. Travel is educa-
tional. I wanna help support your travels. I want you to see my
hometown where I was born, Catania. I want you to take a nice,
easy trip, down through Italy, and when you get to Catania, I
want you to drop in and see my mama. I want you to tell her her
boy is feelin good. And I want you to pick up one of her salamis
for me. Nobody makes salami like mama. And when you get it
I want you to take a plane back here to Paris with it before it
spoils. As a favor between old friends. I pay expenses. And more.
A lot more. For time lost from—he put his foot on my notebook
—this crap.

Not interested Ruby.

Not interested. All right you're not interested. Maybe you be
interested in one of our other businesses. What'd you think we
are we're business men, just like anyone else. There's no law in
business. When you can't do something with a lawyer you do it
with a gun. That's free enterprise. And when you get what you
want incorporate and contribute to charities. That's the way it
works. You know Ronnie we're really on the same side of the
fence. Outsiders. The underworld. Underdogs. Join the underground, get into some big money for once. You start making a
good living, you find a nice girl, you get married, raise bambini,
that's the way to do. Who's that big German dame you shack up
with?

Who says I'm shacking up?

Kem on I know a shackup when I see one. Pair a tits on her
she's worth a lot a dough your Kraut chick, you know that? The
Arabs got the hots for German dames. What a you care about
another Nazi, it's a chance to get even. You slip a pill in her beer,
next thing you know she wakes up in a harem in Yemen with
her legs spread. Pair a tits on her. Come on Ronnie, we can
work something out. What a you wanna go back to the States in
that same old hole? Ain't you sick a that bush-league stuff? You
got money in your pocket, you want something, you buy it. You
run your life the way you want. It just takes a little guts, that's all.

Voici le temps des assassins, I thought. I was sick of my in-
capacity. I thought of Sade Rimbaud Verlaine Lautréamont Jarry
Cendrars Artaud Genet.

What about that shack? There's no rush. Wait until you get tired of her.

She's just a kid I said.

Good. The younger the better. Kids are worth more. You think about it Ronnie. Pair a tits on her. We can work something out. And keep that bill. That's a present. Between old friends.

Ruby left. I sat down at my escritoire and looked out through the court. Harmony, order. The obelisk, stolen from Egypt, the Arc a monument to sheer power, the Etoile itself a grand plan for clearing multiple trajectories for the emperor's canon in case the population should rise. That's order. Too bad about Irmenfrida. I was going to miss her. And besides it was a kind of ratty thing to do to a girl if you really thought about it. Still who knows some girls like that kind of stuff. It's exotic, there's a lot of adventure to it, it involves travel. Irmenfrida loved to travel, like all Germans she was a tourist at heart. And besides she didn't want to go home any more than I did and like me she knew she couldn't stay in Paris where we existed, as I said in a story at the time, like two abstractions whose intersection created their own reality. She had an incipient rape complex anyway, all women do. And she was a big girl she could take a lot of fucking. She'd probably get to like it. I could give her the right orientation, take her to see Rudolph Valentino in *The Sheik,* buy her a copy of *The Story of O*. In any case it would be a good way of terminating our relationship, which couldn't last forever after all. The final solution. For her. But what about me? It wasn't long before Sergeant GunCannon turned up.

Ronnie, this time you're really in trouble. We know every move Ruby makes. We know he's been here. He's walking around with a roll of marked bills. And the minute we catch up with one of those bills, Ruby is finished. We know you made a deal with him. I could pull you in right now on suspicion. A little routine questioning. He cracked his knuckles. But I'm not going to. Because I'm glad you made a deal with Geranium. And you know why I'm glad? Because now we got you where we want you. And you know where we want you? We want you to keep moving. We're gonna keep you moving from Palermo to Yemen to New York to the North End to El Paso, clear back to Old Glory, Arizona, all the way across the country to the Coast. Every city or little hick town where Ruby Geranium's got a contact to make, you're gonna make it, and then you're gonna move on. You're gonna play ball with Ruby Geranium, Ronnie. And every now and then I'm gonna pay you a little visit. Just like old friends. Have fun Ronnie. Be seeing you.

Paris was an abstraction, a theorem, an equation in which I was the unknown term. In the algebra of my fate it had nothing to do with Sergeant GunCannon or Ruby Geranium. It was exempt from my consciousness, and that was why I liked it. The escritoire was Directoire. Paris was a museum, a playground. I was on the lam. Get your kicks. Keep moving. Outside it's twenty degrees. The night is black despite the snow on the ground. The limit of my vision by the light going through the window is the snow-capped rocks of the low wall marking the nearer field. It looks like one of those New England walls from behind which minutemen fought. George Washington crosses the Delaware on the walls. It's amusing how the Colonial decor strike it's amusing how the decor of this Colonial house gives me an illusion of safety. The Sleeping Gypsy, my contribution, sleeps, or rots, the lion waits, and I wonder what happens when and if he wakes up. A remark someone made about me the other day: When you walk into a place—I was walking with him into a place—everybody turns and looks, so that I find myself deciding whose side I'm going to be on when the lynch mob comes. They know you don't play the game. What game? Now we go to my apartment on the Lower East Side of Manhattan, where I wound up in '60, and that I still call home. Now this is where we get to the point, this is where the real story takes place. What story? I was sitting at my desk one day, my wife was out, my girlfriend strike my wife was out. The desk itself is interesting, two rounded curves sweeping out from the back and scooping in at front so you had the sense of the desk wrapping around you, enveloping you as you sat at it, very baroque, curved rows of drawers on either side with many intricate little fascinating compartments in them. And yet it wasn't a frivolous desk, but heavy, massive, solid, and with a surface of labyrinthine grained veneer that I had refinished myself. As I say I was sitting at my desk, the noise came up through the courtyard, clamored along Avenue B. The weather wasn't worth looking at or thinking about, smog followed by soot. But Ruby Geranium had been on my mind again. I thought I finally knew what to do about Ruby Geranium. So I developed the following dialogue with Sergeant GunCannon.

Sergeant, I want to make a deal with you about Ruby Geranium.

We don't make deals Ronnie. What is it?

The other day Ruby came around asking a lot of questions about you. He knows I know you, he knows you're after him. Now I'm sick of this, I want to get you both off my neck. I just want to be left alone. So here's what I'm going to do. I'm going to put you in touch with Ruby. I'm going to arrange a little meeting. I'm going to tell him that you're open to influence.

Now wait a minute Ronnie.

Don't worry Sergeant, I thought of everything. I go up to GunCannon talking quickly under my breath. You wait till he offers you a bribe, then you clap the cuffs on him. I'm the witness. Smart, huh?

Not so fast Ronnie. I gotta think about this.

Too late Sergeant, Ruby Geranium is waiting in the next room. I thought of everything. I open the door. Come on in Ruby. Much to my surprise, Ruby walks right up to GunCannon and shakes his hand.

Eh goombah.

How's the boy Ruby. Hey says GunCannon, your friend here wants me to turn you in for trying to bribe an officer.

Ah forget this jerk says Ruby. He don't know how it works. He holds his five jewel-loaded fingers in front of his chin and gestures at me. Hey, jerk, why doncha learn how it works? he says, grinning. Then he closes his fingers into a fist, and he stops grinning. GunCannon cracks his knuckles. Why don't we teach him how it works says Ruby. Let's play cops and robbers. I bribe you, you arrest me. He reaches into his pocket and grunting pulls out a huge roll of bills. He licks his thumb, counts off five, and looks up at GunCannon. GunCannon looks off into space. He doesn't see anything. All right a little extra today says Ruby. In honor of our friend the jerk. He counts off another three bills, pulls them off the roll, and folds them up. GunCannon doesn't see anything. He turns around and gazes out the window, but his huge hand is stuck out behind him, palm open. Ruby drops the

folded bills into the hand. They disappear. All right says Ruby.
Arrest me.

Arrest you says GunCannon. For what?

For trying to bribe an officer.

Ah come on Ruby. You can't bribe no officers. Officers are too
honest to be bribed. You know that.

Ah gee come on Sergeant, arrest me.

Okay Geranium. You're under arrest.

You'll never get me alive says Ruby. He pulls his hand out of
his pocket and shapes his thumb and forefinger into a gun. But
GunCannon, too quick for him, already has his forefinger aimed
and his thumb cocked. Bang bang you're dead says GunCannon.

Ya got me says Ruby. Hah hah hah he rumbles.

Hah hah hah echoes GunCannon. He laughs like a car trying
to start on a cold morning.

How about that says Ruby. Don't that look like the real thing.

Sure it's the real thing says GunCannon. I know how it works.
Don't forget, I used to be in the movies.

Okay I'm tired of this I said. I still have that marked bill you
strike I still have that bill you gave me in Paris. That marked
bill, remember Ruby? Geranium and GunCannon looked at one
another. I told you I think of everything I said.

You're not going to sing says Geranium.

Come on Ronnie says GunCannon. Why ruin a good thing?
We'll cut you in.

Sure says Geranium. We're all in the same boat.

We just follow orders says GunCannon.

We just do what the big boys tell us says Geranium.

We take our money and keep quiet says GunCannon. Like
anyone else.

Why do ya wanna go and spoil everything says Geranium.

They'll let us die says GunCannon. If you're not useful they
let you die.

They'll kill us says Geranium. You get in the way they kill ya.

Beat it I told them, just like that. Beat it. The story's over.
The game is up.

GunCannon cracked his knuckles. Geranium held up his
barbaric jeweled fist. We'll be back said GunCannon. And they
disappeared.

The droplets rain from the eaves. The shadow of a cloud dims the snow dazzle. George Washington crosses the Delaware on the walls. I sit at my desk, making this up, and keep an eye on the road, waiting for a car to come cruising around the curve, a shiny black Cadillac, an anonymous four-door sedan. A gunshot echoes through the distance. They'll be back. Against that day prepare.

You sit at your desk, you look down at the slum. You begin to understand how it works. Or you drown in it.

People are on your side or they're not. You make contacts, compare notes. It helps you to breathe. Let's not suffocate in our own experience.

They'll be back, are already here, always with me. A gunshot echoes through the distance. The gypsy wakes, if he's still alive, faces the lion, and picks up his lute.

Start with immediate situation. One scene after another, disparate, opaque, absolutely concrete. Later, a fable, a gloss, begins to develop, abstractions appear. End with illuminating formulation. Simple, direct utterance.

A gunshot echoes through the distance.

They'll be back, are already here, always with us.

"The communication of our experience to others is the elemental act of civilization."

They're coming for you.

What's your story?

THE BIRDS

The the the
                Nuthatch walks up the tree a Prussian soldier
pivots walks back down

                                                birds

        the

                  Nuthatch slick arctic acrobat seal bullets through
blank air silence of page the stream carries mainly on its glassy
surface rippled clouds inventing themselves from minute to
minute toss in a stone

The the I want to tell you the story about "ear-tree." It was on
Icelandic that eighteen-hour flight from Luxemburg where your
feet swell up. We cruised among fantastic shapes, formations
piling shifting flowing, distortions of distortions of distortions
at all altitudes. The plane skimmed across a kind of ocean of
streaming transformations, the wings clipped white tumuli, and
on the actual ocean waves were ripples were wrinkles, viscid
metal crawling across the earth, the land itself a slower lava,
somewhat thicker, especially that of Iceland, where that was what
it was. I was looking out over the wing as I watched a wisp
of white blew back from the engine, then another, another,
and after a pause, a band of grey I looked up the aisle for

155

the stewardess when I looked back the smoke was roiling
from the engine a greasy black plume with suddenly red at its
root . . .

Wings pulled in it allowed itself to fall, a stroke of
scarlet from green to green.

It began in '62 a Chinese restaurant
naturally midtown I remember very well because that was the
phase when I had a thing with fortune cookies I am always interested in any overt confrontation

with chance though if you stop
to think about it every moment is such a confrontation for each
of us as likely to provide the cue for something tasty an

adventure
something other than sex a coincidence in any case one was tired
of sex I mean of thinking about it preferably a

coincidence such
things renew my faith in the unknown however the fortune merely
said, "You will soon plan another oriental meal" but that wasn't
the interesting thing.

Corrosive chatter. Starlings are a bore,
despite iridescences. They're too precocious, and have no intelligence. "We put the snake live into the freezer it was at least two
feet long and when we took it out it was frozen into this really
interesting shape stiff as a board but then we hung it up and it
began to smell. What ever happened to Phillip Morris? And
mockies? There always used to be a lot of mockies. I had an
aunt who always used to smoke Phillip Morris. She got lung
cancer though. She was a mockie. She's dead now. I guess that's
what happens to them."

The Yellow-shafted Flicker appears
around April. The male has a black "mustache." Its strange laugh
haunts the woods but seems to be a courtship cry. Lovemaking
involves reciprocal undulations of the long necks like oriental
dancers. The underwing is an astonishing pink-gold. Note the
pure white rump in flight.

The dress was made of clinging white
nylon jersey of a thinness that in certain angles of light would
outline the thighs or reveal the curve of a breast and which, when
taut against the skin, assumed something of the warm flesh tone.
The loose ankle-length curtain of skirt was slit at the side to the

top of the thigh. The backless halter scooped down to the point
at which the swell and division of the buttocks become apparent,
and was slashed to the waist in front, baring both the inner and
outer curves of the breasts, leaving the nipples free to poke and
bob through the material.

"A pattern was seen in the use of fe-
males to bite and kick the policemen" *New York Times* 5/7/68.

Its drumming, distinct from other peckers, resembles the sound
of a muffled machine gun, a soft, hollow automatic weapon.

He
came stumbling up in Tompkins Square with his red scabby face
and clapped a hand on my shoulder: "Say buddy I'm a junkie no
I mean not a junkie a wino." That was how I met Sparrow. Oh
nobody knew what his name really was we called him Sparrow.
After the saying, "Hot as a Sparrow." He used to say things to
me like, "The salient fact about American culture is that we all
have to get back to nipples and start over again. Whole cock-
amanie country." He's also the one who said, "I wuz-a fuck 'is-a
wife." When he talked like that we used to call him "the Cardinal"
because he seemed so intellectual. Like a Cardinal I mean, if you
really look at one.

With one stroke rose half an arc then wings
pulled in allowed itself to fall like diving over a wave.

I want to
write a story that does a lot of infolding and outfolding. Majestic
infolding and outfolding. No petty invective and venom. No
comic bits, no noodgy satire like Shawanga Lodge casino. Calm,
slow exfoliations. The life cycle of Whistling Swans. Inexorable
curves of passion. Rise and fall of continents. Concrete. Innocent.
Beautiful. No meaning.

30 million Americans living in poverty
it says in I. F. Stone
in the richest country in the world
people eat clay to still the pains of an empty belly
children come to school too hungry to learn
and the infants of the poor suffer
irreversible brain damage from protein deprivation
the 42.7% of our farmers
with incomes of less than $2,500 a year
received only 4.5% of total farm subsidies

while the top 10%
many of them farm corporations or vertical trusts
received 64.5%
with a budget allocated 80% to the Pentagon
and 10% to health education and welfare

This is what I call pure poetry. This is the New American Poetry, the poetry of pure fact. This is the purity that has been missing from our poems.

Red-winged Blackbirds floating in like Piper Cubs, suns on shoulders. Phoebe brooding on her egg. Towhee, Picasso camouflage, comic butler in tails. Catbird chat. Brown Thrasher variations. Oriole riff. Pheasants waltz across the road. In the field a Crow barks. A Hawk hangs in the air, absolutely still. Grouse explode in the underbrush. Doves at their vespers. Invisible, huge in the night sky, a train of Canada Geese goes honking and gabbling full five minutes from engine to caboose.

There was an item on the menu and the Chinese was translated as "Ear-tree." It was right between Shar Ding Op (chickens, Chinese frankfurter, water chestnut) and Hong Hong Duk (lobster nails, pig flesh, Chinese vegetable). Myself I was all for getting the "Ten Ingredient." I felt expansive and experimental. But Phoebe, who was a big girl, tended toward "Mile High Rice," with maybe an order of "Stopped Duck," or "Blistered Beef," whatever that was. So then we asked ourselves, well, what would "the Sparrow" do? Our eyes met for an instant. There was no doubt about it: "Ear-tree." We didn't even have to speak.

"Seen as how I'm a nice guy, I'll give you a tip. We like to stop guys with long hair, especially in old cars. They look like students. You're a teacher. Teach and be taught."

I put the ticket in my pocket. "Yeah. Well I didn't know driving with studded snow tires was illegal in this state after May first as of ten days ago." I opened my car door.

"Hey. Come 'ere."

I walked back to the patrol car.

"It's not illegal."

"No?"

"No. It's unlawful."

"Oh."

I walked back to my car and opened the door.

"Hey. Come 'ere."

I walked back to the patrol car.

"Ya know what illegal is?"

"No, what?"

"It's a sick bird. Hah hah hah."

Q. When does a bird break the law?

A. When it's a Robin.

Q. What characteristic distinguishes the Bald Eagle?

A. Its balls.

Q. When is a bird not a bird?

A. When it's a horse.

> poor Americans are four times as likely to die
> before the age of 35 as the average citizen
> Negro women in Mississippi die
> six times as often in childbirth as white women
> in some urban ghettos of the North
> one child in ten dies in infancy
> the health gap between rich and poor is growing
> in 1940 the infant mortality rate for non-whites
> was 70% higher than that for whites
> in 1962 the rate was 90% greater
> the life expectancy of an American Negro is 61 years
> that of a white American
> is 68
> it says
> in the *Sunday*
> *Times*

The Downy Woodpecker, in his prison outfit, is easily confused with the Hairy, which in fact is almost identical. However the Downy is smaller than the Hairy, and its call, *pik*, is softer than Hairy's. The Black-capped Chickadee is the friendliest of acrobats. The Bobwhite is a gallinaceous bird, very henny in other words, and acts it. But let us ascend from the ridiculous to the majestic. The Whistling Swan is common. It has a wingspan of over seven feet. Like other swans, it has a "deep, ponderous flight," neck extended. When swimming neck is stiff and straight; secondaries are not raised.

Q. What bird would you be glad to see if you were out of gas?

A. The Petrel.
Q. What birds can't fly straight?
A. Terns.
Q. What birds are often run over by trains?
A. Rails.
Q. What bird's ass would you not want to sit on?
A. The Pintail's.
Q. Which-a bird is not-a yours-a?
A. Myna.
Q. When does a bird make a sacrifice?
A. When it's a Bunting.
Q. What bird blows his whistle?
A. Old Dickcissel, old Dickcissel.

                                                    birds

                    the

                                        what do they say

through the empty air
                                        keep-back keep-back

peter-peter-peter
                                        tea-cher tea-cher

o-say mari-a
                                        hurry worry flurry blurry

drink-your-tea drink-your-tea
                                        old sam peabodypeabodypeabody

ticket-ticket-ticket-ticket
                                        wide-a-wake

rounde-lay rounde-lay
                                        trees trees if you please

witchery-witchery-witchery
                                        whip-three-beers

chicky-tucky-tuck
                                        chicky-tucky-tuck

We are all, of course, familiar with that kind of anthropomor-
phic slop. What do the birds really say when you listen hard and
understand what they are saying? They say k-a-a-a. They say
kwrrk. They say

	kow-kow-kow	
keeur		kleep
	kzrrt	
prrrp		bzee
	plick	
rronk		tlu-tlu
	krr-oww	
zrurrr		wheet
	peent	
tsweep		cuh-cuh
	churree	
che-bunk		kraaa
	che-bek	
jeet		hooah
	tschizzik	
kirrik		ssllick
	karr-reek	
kwuririp		kek-kek-kek
	kee-oo	
auw		churweeoo
	ooah-ooo-oo-oo	
pchip ee pcheewee		breep

But then again, what does it matter what they say? What
matters is that they carve shapes from nothingness, decorate the
silence, make melodious distinctions to distinguish one moment
finely from the next.
                      I call waiter. What thisee here, I say. He say,
That is "ear-tree," a delicious Oriental specialty. But Phoebe no
likee. What is? she ask. She little girl, no muchee eatee. "Ear-tree"
is a popular and delicious Cantonese dish, say waiter. He Chinee
fella. It is highly recommended, he say. But what is? I say. Waiter
shrug and stare to other sidee room with inscrutable Chinee face.
No likee, Phoebe say. You got Chicken Chow Mein. Waiter nod.
I order Chop Suey. Then other customer come. They order "ear-

tree." Waiter go in kitchen, we hear yellee to cook: Two spag-
hettis! I callee waiter. What this "ear-tree," I say. I pointee at
menu. You say is Canton dish. Then waiter answer: It doesn't
matter what you say. What matters is to hurl the words at the
silence of the page like hand grenades. With feeling. Look out!
someone screamed. He's got a gun!

         "But why 'ear-tree'?" asked
Phoebe, wide-eyed. She was a slim, light-haired pale face on
summer vacation from Bryn Mawr College, but with very big
boobs.

 "Ah, these ees the ow-you-say question my young chérie," answered Sparrow. She was at the same time flattered and offended
by his insistence that she use his first name, for it implied both a
compliment and an impropriety. Why, she wondered, as she
stared out the porthole and watched the clouds transform themselves from moment to moment, feeling the touch of his shark-
skin on her bare microskirted thigh, did her parents allow a trip
to Europe in the company of this strange, dark, manly business
acquaintance of her father's, with his profile, his greying side-
burns, and his carriage and skin texture that reminded her so
much of an erect cock? She quivered a bit in her seat, and fas-
tened her safety belt. He was mainly Latin in descent, from a
Franco-Italian Spanish family with an intermixture of Greco-
Moorish blood, that settled on the island of Malta some centuries
ago in the wake of the conquest of Jerusalem. Sparrow. Spiro?
Ero? She wondered if it was his real name. He was the kind of
person that might be incognito. The jetliner shuddered through a
cumulonimbus. She pulled a lever easing her seat into a reclining
position that thrust her long full firm young thighs up and forward
from the pelvis where the thin stuff of her microgarb caught and
bunched under her seatbelt.

 "But why 'ear-tree'?" asked Phoebe.

 "My charming eediot," rejoined his vibrant basso, "if we knew
these . . ." His middle and index fingers grazed her thigh confi-
dentially, and came to rest near the hem of her skirt. She pre-
tended not to notice, since she didn't know what else to do, and
turned to look through the porthole where she saw a sheep
running across the wing, no not a sheep a puff of smoke, another,
another then after a pause a band of grey a plume of roiling
black with suddenly red at its root . . .

"Built entirely without design precedent or orderly planning, created bit by bit on sheer impulse, a natural artist's instinct, and the fantasy of the moment": Simone Rodia's Watts Towers. Connections proliferate, meanings drop away.

Sparrow left England traveling as a young Greek sailor named George and Nick. I found him easily before the ship had cleared harbor leaning against the starboard rail in tight white pants and striped blue shirt. The day was blue with white clouds, whitecaps, gulls dove and hung above the churning stern. The gulls of Dover scream like Harpies and fly on wings of rusty iron. Sparrow was traveling as a young Greek sailor named George and Nick, but he spoke with a thick Italian accent. " 'owza da boy?" he greeted me. His theory was that from his Italian accent he would be taken for a notorious Neapolitan intellectual known as "the Cardinal" who was inclined to proletarian dress and argot as a disguise. If however he were recognized as the Greek sailor boy George and Nick masquerading as the Cardinal in proletdrag, he would still be ahead of the game. This was the evasive measure known as bifurcation. While the authorities are interrogating George and Nick, Sparrow slips out between the two of them. Or if they settle on George, Nick sidles off and meantime George subdivides into Sparrow-Spiro-Ero. The principle here is progressive fission as in certain microorganisms. They never catch up with you, whoever you are. But this, ironically, is the hang-up of the method, since some agents have been left stranded in a maze of sloughed identities nursing a king-size identity problem. Often you will see an old hand slap a green agent on the back, wink, and growl avuncularly, "Say kid, what you say we go fission?" This is the process referred to, so beware.

Sparrow pointed toward a couple standing on the bridge next to the skipper, and slipped a homing pigeon out of his attaché case. The man was tall and slender, suntanned, and of a distinguished allure in the French sense. The woman was tall and slender, suntanned, and also of a distinguished allure, etc. At this distance it was a little difficult to tell them apart, though they were both quite distinct from the skipper, who was pale and squat and emanated banality. The bird ruffled and fluttered, happy to escape its confinement. Sparrow set it on his wrist, raised it high in the air, and whispered "Dai! Dai!" The pigeon flapped off while

Sparrow began reciting the Paolo and Francesca episode from the fifth canto of the *Commedia*. We watched as the bird hovered over the woman's head for a moment, then perched on her shoulder. We watched as she reached up and removed the message from the bird's leg, still looking straight ahead. We watched as she swallowed the note, took the pigeon, twisted its neck, and let it flop to the deck. Then the suntanned man was standing alone on the bridge, near the squat skipper, still looking straight ahead. Sparrow pointed to the man and shrugged. "I wuz-a fuck 'iz-a wife," he said in explanation. Just then said lady appeared at the rail near us and stood there looking straight ahead. "Beh!" said Sparrow. Was he as surprised as I was to recognize Phoebe? There was probably no telling. She looked straight ahead, her eyes on the horizon. The gulls dipped and hung in our wake. Sparrow cleared his throat. "Ear-tree," he said. Phoebe turned to him, her charcoal eyes smouldering in her olive face: "Millions of people are starving. A sixth of the population lives in poverty. In the richest nation in the world, in the history of the world. Abroad we practice mass murder, at home slow genocide. How long can we continue to regard as democratic a nation run like a company town for corporate profit, built-in poverty, endemic racism? Starving children suffer irreversible brain damage while Senators get rich. Soldiers die while profits soar. Democracy by tear gas, Mace, and political assassination. What are we going to do?"

"We like to stop guys with long hair and old cars," he said. "First of all old cars are a drug on the market like. I mean seen as how you got an old car it means you ain't got a new car right. And if all you was to pay is a few bucks on an old car you ain't puttin much back into the system are yiz? And that breaks the law of the market which is free enterprise.

"Now we ain't got nothin against long hair see. But what about all these guys that set up shop as barbers, they gotta make their profit, right? That breaks the law of supply and demand.

"Now another thing is long hair ain't neat like. And if it ain't neat it's unruly. And if it's unruly it's unlawful in this state according to a law on the books as of ten days ago by which appearance can be considered an extension of overt behavior during periods of national emergency such as for example now.

"Now seen as how guys with long hair and old cars don't fit in a system for guys with old hair and long cars, what that means is you're a troublemaker which is an offense by the new law that considers mental attitude an extension of overt behavior during times of national emergency 063589 state penal code and authorizes the arresting officer to put certain questions to the accused according to the mental stop-and-search provision on grounds of reasonable suspicion like long hair and old cars. Wrong answers are considered grounds for perjury.

Part I *Short Answer* (10 points)
1. How would you define "illegal"?
2. What characteristic distinguishes the Bald Eagle?
3. When does a bird break the law?
4. What birds can't fly straight?
5. What bird's ass would you not want to sit on?

Part II *Essay* (90 points)
Choose *one* of the following:
   a) This story is "entirely without design precedent or orderly planning, created bit by bit on sheer impulse, a natural artist's instinct, and the fantasy of the moment." Why do you think the police don't like that? Discuss.
   b) What is "ear-tree"? Give examples.
In Part II, I answered b). This was my answer: "Connections proliferate, meanings disperse. The painter studies his nude, his landscape."
         IN A SPIRIT OF JOY AND REVOLUTIONARY EXULTATION, THOUSANDS OF STUDENTS OCCUPIED THE SORBONNE TODAY.
      THE STUDENTS STARTED MOVING INTO THE UNIVERSITY LATE LAST NIGHT, AFTER COMPLETING THEIR JOINT PROTEST MARCH WITH THE WORKERS OF PARIS AND SPENDING THE EVENING DANCING ON THE COBBLED STREETS OF THE LATIN QUARTER.
      IN THE GRANDIOSE COBBLED COURTYARD OF THE MAIN BUILDING A SMALL JAZZ BAND PLAYED ALL THROUGH THE NIGHT.
      AFTER 10 DAYS OF BLOODY CLASHES WITH THE POLICE, NOT A SINGLE POLICEMAN WAS IN SIGHT. STU-

DENTS IN WHITE HELMETS DIRECTED TRAFFIC. THE
GOVERNMENT HAD SURRENDERED THIS PART OF
THE CITY TO THE STUDENTS.

HUNDREDS OF THOUSANDS OF STUDENTS TOOK TO
THE STREETS NOT ONLY IN PARIS BUT IN MOST PRO-
VINCIAL CITIES.

MANY HAD A FEAR THAT GOVERNMENTAL POWER
HAD BROKEN DOWN.

THE STUDENTS THEMSELVES DELIBERATELY
HARKED BACK TO THE BATTLE CRIES THAT HAD
SERVED EARLIER FRENCH REVOLUTIONARIES.

TWO THOUSAND WORKERS, IMITATING THE RE-
BELLIOUS STUDENTS OF THE SORBONNE, HAVE OC-
CUPIED THE AIRCRAFT CONSTRUCTION PLANT OF
SUD-AVIATION AT NANTES, ON THE ATLANTIC
COAST, AND ARE HOLDING THE PLANT MANAGER
AND HIS PRINCIPAL AIDES PRISONERS.

THE WORKERS, WHO WERE ALREADY ON STRIKE,
MOVED INTO THE PLANT EARLY LAST NIGHT AND
WELDED THE MAIN GATE CLOSED. THEY THREW UP
BARRICADES ON THE ROADS LEADING TO THE
PLANT. THEY CLOSED DOWN THE NANTES AIRPORT,
WHICH IS ADJACENT TO THE FACTORY.

FRANCE'S SOCIAL REVOLT SPREAD AND CHANGED
IN NATURE TODAY AS AN ESTIMATED 100,000 STRIK-
ERS OCCUPIED DOZENS OF FACTORIES IN ALL PARTS
OF THE COUNTRY.

THE STRIKE MOVEMENT SPREAD SO SWIFTLY
THAT, WITHIN HALF AN HOUR EARLY THIS EVENING,
REPORTS REACHED PARIS THAT SEVEN MAJOR IN-
DUSTRIAL PLANTS AND SHIPYARDS HAD BEEN
TAKEN OVER IN LE HAVRE ALONE.

PRODUCERS AND DIRECTORS OF THE GOVERN-
MENT'S TELEVISION AND RADIO SYSTEM WENT ON
STRIKE AND THE SYSTEM'S NEWSMEN VOTED TO RE-
FUSE TO ACCEPT ANY FURTHER DIRECTIVES FROM
THE INFORMATION MINISTRY OR OTHER GOVERN-
MENT AGENCIES ON THEIR NEWS REPORTS.

WORKERS SEIZED THE GOLD-DOMED OPERA AND
THE OPERA COMIQUE.

THE SPEECHES AT THE NATIONAL ASSEMBLY SEEMED STRANGELY IRRELEVANT. FRANCOIS MITTERAND, THE OPPOSITION LEADER, AND WALDECK ROCHET, THE HEAD OF THE COMMUNIST PARTY, WERE AS HOPELESSLY OUT OF TOUCH AS PREMIER GEORGES POMPIDOU. THEY WERE ALL PART OF THE "ESTABLISHMENT."

ONE OF THE STUDENT LEADERS, DANIEL COIN-BENDIT, CALLED THE COMMUNISTS "STALLINIST CREEPS." MR. COHN-BENDIT, CALLED DANNY THE RED, APPEARS TO HOLD VIEWS CLOSE TO ANARCHISM.

THE BLACK FLAG OF THE ANARCHISTS MADE ITS APPEARANCE DURING THE MASSIVE PARADE OF STUDENTS AND WORERS YEKSTERDAY.

THE RED FLAG WAS HOISTED OVER SEVERAL PLANTS.

THE RED AND THE BLACK FLAGS APPEARED TOGETHER, AN ABNORMAL SITUATION BECAUSE THE COMMUNISTS AND ANARCHISTS HAVE LONG BEEN ENEMIES. THE JOINT APPEARANCE WAS ONE OF THE MANY SIGNS THAT SOMETHING NEW HAD HAPPENED.

IF THE MOVEMENT IS AN UNCONTROLLED REVOLUTIONARY UPSURGE, THE COUNTRY MAY BE PLUNGED INTO ANARCHY.

THE DECISION OF THE WORKERS APPEARS TO HAVE BEEN A SPONTANEOUS MOVE BY THE RANK-AND-FILE STRIKERS, WHO ACTED WITHOUT ORDERS FROM POLITICAL PARTIES OR LABOR UNIONS.

THE STUDENT REVOLT WAS SIMILARLY UNOFFICIAL IN ITS ORIGIN.

IT IS THIS POPULAR AND REVOLUTIONARY CHARACTER OF THE MOVEMENT THAT LEADS MANY OBSERVERS TO FEEL THAT THE STUDENTS MAY HAVE UNLEASHED FORCES THAT CANNOT BE HARNESSED OR TAMED BY CONVENTIONAL MEANS, EITHER BY THE GOVERNMENT OR THE TRADITIONAL OPPOSITION PARTIES, INCLUDING THE COMMUNISTS.

JUST WHAT CAUSED THE STUDENTS' AND WORKERS'

REVOLT TO ASSUME SUCH EXPLOSIVE DIMENSIONS
IS STILL A MYSTERY TO MOT OBSERVER HERE.

MANY HAVE LINKED THE DISILLUSION OF THE
FRENCH STUDENT TO A GLOBAL STUDENT MALAISE.

THE GAULLIST ADMINISTRATION, LIKE MANY PRI-
VATE CITIZENS, IS CONVINCED THAT A TRULY REVO-
LUTIONARY SITUATION EXISTS AND THAT THE
DEMOCRATIC INSTITUTIONS OF FRANCE ARE
THREATENED.

THE PRINCIPAL THREAT LIES IN THE SPONTA-
NEOUS, POPULAR AND UTTERLY UNCONTROLLED
NATURE OF THE MOVEMENT.

THE REVOLT, BY ITS SPONTANEOUS, TOTALLY UN-
CONTROLLED AND UNCONTROLLABLE NATURE HAD
BECOME A TRULY REVOLUTIONARY EVENT.

IF THE COMMUNIST PARTY HAS MANAGED TO
TAKE OVER THE MOVEMENT, THEN, IRONICALLY,
THE INSTITUTIONS ARE SAFE AND THE POLITICAL
CONTEST IS LIKELY TO MOVE BACK INTO THE NA-
TIONAL ASSEMBLY, WITH VOTES OF CONFIDENCE
AND VOTES OF CENSURE AND TRADITIONAL
SPEECHES—AND SOONER OR LATER A NEW ELEC-
TION.

SOMETHING HAS BEEN CREATED THAT IS IRRE-
VERSIBLE. THERE WILL BE NO GOING BACK TO THE
STATUS QUO.

　　　　　　　　The police want an end to this disorder and that
depends on one question and one question only: What is "ear-
tree"? This in turn leads us to the matter of the identity of the
man called "Ero." Destroy this as you read. It is printed in a sol-
uble ink which you can lick off the page sentence by sentence.
The ink has various flavors depending on the parts of speech to
make this easier to understand and swallow.

To get to the point, the police suspect a plot, yet all they see
is disorder. They suspect that disorder is part of the plot, if
not the point of it. They imagine that they merely have to figure
out the plot to put an end to the disorder. But they don't understand the plot and believe the explanation lies with the meaning of the word "ear-tree." In turn they believe that this meaning will lead them to a man called Ero. In real life Ero is an

eminent ornithologist, but the police believe that he is the leader
of an international liberation conspiracy, and that only in his
mind are all the connections coherently held together, the whole
matter fully understood. To make matters worse, they aren't
even sure whether Ero is dead or alive, or for that matter whether
that is his right name.

I first met Ero in Tompkins Square Park. He was disguised as
a bum. Although he was given to a kind of banal chattering—he
sometimes compared himself to a Starling—I soon realized that
this was a mere verbal subterfuge, so to speak, which could not
prevent the escape of sudden flashes of the profoundest insight.
For example he once remarked, almost as a non sequitur, that
the whole country had to get back to nipples. It was not long
before I was captivated by his brilliance and charisma. At about
that point I met another of his admirers, an English "bird" named
Phoebe. Though she attended an American college, she was married; however, she had an ambiguous relation with her husband,
and while she traveled with him a good deal, she spent much of
the time in the protection of her parents. Ero once indicated to
me quite clearly that there had been something between them,
but then, she was beautiful and he—he was Ero.

To continue, at that time Phoebe and I used to frequent Chinese restaurants. That was because it used to be Ero's way to
plant his messages in fortune cookies and leave strictly to chance
whether you received them or not—Ero favored chance because
he said we must remain open to the unknown. They say that he
still does this, and that you might for all you know receive a
message from him yourself in your very next fortune cookie—a
message that might change your life. Anyway we were sitting in
this Cantonese place in midtown, speaking Pigeon English to put
the natives at ease and to confuse the police. The waiter recommended "ear-tree"—could he have been Ero?—but when he
ordered it for someone else called it "spaghetti."

At first I thought that "ear-tree" had something to do with
birds—a kind of tree that birds liked to sing in, or to. Ero was of
course filled with bird lore. Birds were something special for him.
He said that bird songs constituted a kind of code which, when
correctly deciphered, turned out to have absolutely no meaning.
On the other hand he had a whole system of private symbolism
worked out on the basis of what the various species meant to him,

and would often express himself in its terms. This was a code
the police never cracked, though God knows they tried. For
example, he once sent me a message composed completely of bird
images. These involved the Red-winged Blackbird, the Phoebe,
the Rufous-sided Towhee, the Catbird, the Brown Thrasher, the
Oriole (Orchard), the Pheasant, the Crow, the Hawk, the Grouse,
the Dove, the Canada Goose, in that order. Knowing his system
based on his emotional response to different birds, I worked the
symbols out as follows:

> Red-winged Blackbird = calm dash
> Phoebe = domestic
> Rufous-sided Towhee = human comedy
> Catbird = eccentric relativism
> Brown Thrasher = rich
> Oriole (Orchard) = hot butter
> Pheasant = beautiful fortune, pathetic sacrifice
> Crow = wisdom floats intensely
> Hawk = kill with grace
> Grouse = explosion
> Dove = dumb animals
> Canada Goose = away, away

Decoded and allowing for variation in the given images in which
the birds appeared, this means, roughly: "The *calm dash* of our
once *domestic* culture has faded along with our old *human
comedy*. In its place we have an *eccentric relativism* that is as
rich as experience itself, yet as slippery as *hot butter*. Today's
tragic hero is a man of *beautiful fortune, pathetic sacrifice*—his
role as rich as the flux itself, and his denouement as meaningless.
But in this streaming chaos *wisdom floats intensely* could one but
be deadly enough with the fine net of intelligence. For wisdom
and art mean precisely to kill the quick of our experience as it
races past, but to *kill with grace* so that the victim may be pre-
served, as if alive, from oblivion. The universe is a long, an infinite *explosion* in which we are driven for an instant like *dumb
animals* as it rushes *away, away*."

Unfortunately, when I showed this interpretation to Ero, he
got very angry and tore it up. When I asked what his system of
bird symbolism meant to him he replied: "Nothing. A feather here
and there, a color, a squawk, disconnected, opaque, totally self-

contained, ending in a triumph of birdness, song and soar, itself
opaque and without equivalent, but the feeling ordered and de-
fined—like that of a bird's song, or of its flight."

That was my last encounter with Ero, as such. Immediately
after that he assumed the guise of Spiro the spy, then of the
Cardinal, then of George and Nick, and then literally disappeared
in a welter of dividing and subdividing identities—Orson, Chet
Nexus, the Beach Boy, Madame Lafayette, the Light-fingered
Trio—to name just a few. Originally intended as an evasive
measure against an assassination plot, this frenzy of transformations, some believe, may have made him a victim of terminal
identity fission, a malignant psychological disorder which progressively rarefies the ego so that it ultimately loses consciousness
of itself and in effect ceases to exist. Some say that he was seized
and murdered in one of his ephemeral metamorphoses—thrown
overboard by the squat skipper and the pimply homosexual
second mate as George and Nick, on board a plane that crashed in
mysterious circumstances off Iceland, shot dead in a Chinese restaurant by a Cuban exile who ordered "ear-tree" and got spaghetti.
No one really knows.

What we do now know definitely, or at least what I know and
you will in thirty seconds, is the meaning of "ear-tree." Shhh. It
was on Icelandic that eighteen-hour flight from Luxemburg where
your feet swell up when the insight came to me. Three A.M. and I
couldn't sleep. We had been traveling maybe nine, ten hours.
Nothing could have been further from my mind than that old
riddle. I leaned back against my pillow and thought *oreiller*,
French for pillow. I had been in France. Then I thought *pommier*,
apple tree, *cerisier*, cherry tree, *pêcher*, peach tree, *oranger*,
orange tree. Then I thought *oreille*, ear. Then I thought voila!
oreiller, "ear-tree." But why "ear-tree" on a Chinese menu? Of
course! Spaghetti. In Chinese restaurants in France, *lo-mein*,
which as we know was brought from China to Italy as *spaghetti*,
is often called *pilaf* or *pilaw*, from the Arabic, because it is used
as a pillow for some kind of ragout or sauce. So some Chinese
who knew neither French nor English nor Arabic very well,
translated *lo-mein* to *pilaw*, *pilaw* to *oreiller*, and *oreiller* from
French to English as "ear-tree." I immediately dropped off into a
profound slumber from which I awoke next morning completely
refreshed.

When I arrived in New York, I went back to that same Chinese restaurant and ordered a large "ear-tree." It was of excellent quality, at least three stars, and I polished it off with tremendous satisfaction. The message in my fortune cookie read: "Connections proliferate, meanings are dispelled. The traveler studies out his map."

"Je suis réellement désolé I'm really sorry to have waited so long before answering you but I am totally caught up in the events that have taken place in May and in June in France. You've undoubtedly had some echoes but it's difficult to imagine the extraordinary enthusiasm that sustained the young people during the month of May."

"To form a perfect conception of the beauty and elegance of these Swans, you must observe them when they are not aware of your proximity . . . the neck, which at other times is held stiffly upright, moves in graceful curves . . . with a sudden effort a flood of water is thrown over the back and wings, when it is seen rolling off in sparkling globules, like so many large pearls. The bird then shakes its wings, beats the water, and as if giddy with delight shoots away, gliding . . . with surprising agility and grace. Imagine, reader, that a flock of fifty Swans are thus sporting before you, as they have more than once in my sight, and you will feel, as I have felt, more happy and void of care than I can describe."

The dress was made of clinging white nylon jersey of a thinness that in certain angles of light would outline the thighs or reveal the curve of a breast and which, when taut against the skin, assumed something of the warm flesh tone. Slashed to the waist, it left the nipples free to poke and bob through the material.

in the richest country in the world/ people eat clay to still the pains of an empty belly/ children come to school too hungry to learn/ and the infants of the poor suffer/ irreversible brain damage from protein deprivation

JUST WHAT CAUSED THE STUDENTS' AND WORKERS' REVOLT TO ASSUME SUCH EXPLOSIVE DIMENSIONS IS STILL A MYSTERY TO MOT OBSERVER HERE MANY HAVE LINKED THE DISILLUSION OF THE

FRENCH STUDENT TO A GLOBAL STUDENT MA-
LAISE

Ero is an eminent ornithologist, but the police believe
that he is the leader of an international liberation conspiracy, and
that only in his mind are all the connections coherently held together

"A pattern was seen in the use of females to bite and kick
the policemen" *New York Times* 5/7/68. Its drumming, distinct
from other peckers, resembles the sound of a muffled machine
gun, a soft, hollow automatic weapon.

"Les manifestations sur les
barricades the demonstrations on the barricades were only one
aspect, perhaps secondary, of this surprising movement, much
more astonishing was the climate in the streets. We organized
every day and during the month of May all-day meetings each
of which gathered up to a hundred people sometimes until two in
the morning."

THE REVOLT BY ITS SPONTANEOUS TO-
TALLY UNCONTROLLED AND UNCONTROLLABLE
NATURE HAD BECOME A TRULY REVOLUTIONARY
EVENT

"Spontanément spontaneously, the people raised the
real problems, confusedly felt and it was this, exactly that was
extraordinary—it was not a question of the usual political theo-
ries struggling but of notions as vague as human dignity, the
responsibility of each man, the infinite resources of the emotion
of enthusiasm facing efficiency, the power of technology—"

IF
THE MOVEMENT IS AN UNCONTROLLED REVOLU-
TIONARY UPSURGE THE COUNTRY MAY BE PLUNGED
INTO ANARCHY

"entirely without design precedent or orderly
planning, created bit by bit on sheer impulse"

coincidence such
things renew my faith in the unknown I am always interested in
any overt confrontation with chance though if you stop to think
about it every moment is such a confrontation for each of us Ero
favored chance because he said we must remain open to the
unknown

the stream carries mainly on its glassy surface rippled clouds inventing themselves from minute to minute, fantastic shapes, formations piling shifting flowing, distortions of distortions of distortions

"Nous attendons we await November, December but also the movements that cannot fail to appear in Italy, Germany perhaps the United States . . ."

in the richest country in the world

an international liberation conspiracy

the children of the poor

caused the revolt to assume such explosive

spontaneous totally uncontrolled and uncontrollable

a soft hollow automatic weapon

left the nipples free to poke and bob

much more astonishing was the climate in the streets

a small jazz band played all through the night

the infinite resources of the emotion of enthusiasm

created bit by bit on sheer impulse

we await November December

formations piling shifting flowing

we must remain open to the unknown

the bird then shakes its wings beats the water and shoots away gliding like other Swans it has a deep ponderous flight the underwing is an astonishing pink-gold stroke of scarlet from green to green Nuthatch bullets through blank air Redwinged Blackbirds floating in in the field a Crow barks

Pheasants waltz across the road

Grouse explode in the underbrush

a Hawk

hangs
in the air

birds

the